Evil Chose You

Brilliantly Dark Tales of Terror

Jonathan Jewett

Camlan Press

Edited by Patricia Bull

Cover art and design by Katya Hassett

Print ISBN: 979-8-9894308-2-6

For C + D

Remember to always make friends with the monsters under your bed.

Contents

DRIVE

I.

Will Butler glanced out the living room window at his quiet street while he stuffed paperwork into his briefcase. It was 8:11 and his 8AM Beemo had still not arrived, which was unusual. TRAVEL BEAUTIFULLY, SAFELY, AND ON TIME was their motto, after all, and according to his watch another minute had just clicked by. *Twelve minutes late now.*

Normally he wasn't bothered by minor delays, but today he had a flight to catch and little room for error. Rush-hour traffic was like the weather in Boston: when you didn't know, assume the worst.

He was flying to Chicago today for two days of meetings and was feeling optimistic about the trip. His first meeting that afternoon was with one of the biggest construction companies in the Midwest, and Will fully expected to walk away with a signed contract for almost six-hundred-thousand dollars. Everything had already been negotiated, and they just needed to sign. Now *that* would be a nice commission check. Tonight, he was having dinner with a former colleague who was promising to steer more business his way. "I'm consulting with a couple of clients who really need your software," his guy said, "and if I tell them to buy, they'll buy." Friday's meetings were just as promising, and with a little luck he'd be back in time to coach Zac's flag football game at seven. It was the kind of trip he liked—short, easy and profitable.

The opening bars of the *Miami Vice* TV theme rang out from his phone. *Alison.* "Hi, Hon, just waiting for the evil egg to pick me up. It's running late."

"Hope it gets there soon. Traffic is crazy." Alison had already dropped Zac off at school and was arriving at her office in Downtown Crossing. They had just missed each other that morning and Will could still detect the slightest scent of Eternity in their kitchen. "Just wanted to say have a safe trip. Sending love and good luck with the meetings."

"Thanks. If this works out, we'll be booking that trip to Aruba."

"Mama needs a trip," she laughed. "Go get it for me and call when you get there."

"Will do. Bye." Will cast an eye around to see if he'd forgotten anything, then shut his briefcase and set it by the front door. Small fingers of morning sun reached through the panes and warmed his skin. *Nice day to fly*, he thought. *Sunny and clear.* His eyes wandered across the street to his neighbor's driveway, where Dave's latest automotive mishap sat rotting under a dirty tarp. *What an eyesore.* Will made a mental note to visit Dave for a little chat when he returned from Chicago.

His vibrating phone signaled the Beemo's arrival just as it pulled up to the curb. *Finally.* Tapping the left breast pocket of his sportscoat (*wallet, check)* and then the right (*phone, check*), Will pushed down the ever-present feeling that he'd forgotten something and walked outside to meet his car.

Designed to maximize space and the passenger aesthetic, the Beemo 5200AV resembled a large black egg on wheels. Its tinted and shatterproof windows shone like obsidian mirrors from the outside and offered amazing 360-degree views from the inside, a big part of the car's appeal. When he saw his first Beemo, Will thought it to be an oddity—amusing even—but since then, the robotaxis had swarmed across America's highways like carpenter ants. A journalist had coined the moniker "evil egg" to describe its bizarre and somewhat menacing appearance and the nickname stuck, even becoming a term of affection among aficionados like Will.

Not everyone was pleased with Beemo's rapid expansion, however, and there was vocal opposition to a shadowy technology people saw spreading faster than the social, political, and legal systems could react to it. There were protests and boycotts, widespread vandalism and growing calls for transparency. Other than the Beemo Corporation itself, nobody really knew how the self-driving taxis worked, and the thought of being surrounded by zombie robot cars on a Sunday drive with the family unnerved many people. Beemo's opponents saw the car less as a symbol of progress than as a dangerous new technology being unleashed on an unsuspecting public by a company that prioritized profits over safety. The fact that the company had adopted a public persona as enigmatic as its driverless cars did little to allay the public's fears, and opposing positions had only hardened since Beemo's introduction four years earlier.

Will approached the passenger-side retina scanner. The car made a positive ID and the door flipped open, allowing him entry. Leather seats encircled the car's spacious interior, offering a single passenger like him plenty of room to stretch out and even nap. Will selected a molded leather seat toward the back and snapped his seat belt into place as the door shut and locked securely behind him.

"GOOD MORNING will butler," an automated voice filled the compartment. "THANK YOU FOR DRIVING WITH BEEMO. PLEASE ACCEPT MY APOLOGIES FOR A SLIGHTLY LATE ARRIVAL. THE REASON FOR MY LATENESS IS traffic. WE'LL NOW BE DEPARTING FOR logan airport WITH AN ESTIMAT-

ED ARRIVAL TIME OF eight fifty-eight. THANK YOU FOR FASTENING YOUR SEAT BELT AND PLEASE SIT BACK, RELAX, AND WATCH A BRIEF SAFETY VIDEO WHILE BEEMO GETS YOU THERE BEAUTIFULLY, SAFELY AND ON TIME."

The car pulled from the curb into the street and began to pick up speed, heading southeast toward Boston. Having ignored the mandatory safety video dozens of times, Will instead got comfortable and flipped his laptop open. He relied on Beemo almost exclusively for travel these days, and in his opinion you just couldn't beat it for convenience and the riding experience. Plus, driverless cars meant not having to deal with chatty cabbies. He couldn't stand it when drivers tried to lure him into banal conversation while he just wanted to relax or study his fantasy football lineup. In Will's opinion, it was much better to skip human interaction entirely and let the machine do the driving.

On most days, he could make it to Logan in forty-five minutes. Checking the large display screen in the front right corner of the vehicle, Will could see only one or two flashing red dots signifying traffic along the way. *That's good.* He noticed that the Beemo had chosen a route that avoided the highways and channeled them straight through the city, which usually meant the big roads were snarled with morning commuters. Will didn't mind; the travel time was about the same, and the Mass Pike offered no aesthetics beyond the backsides of dirty buildings and concrete. Driving through Boston in a Beemo was an indulgence, a furtive pleasure. After a 20-plus-year career in sales, he'd grown to appreciate the little things: flights that actually left on time, an empty middle seat next to him or a Beemo ride to the airport. Individually, they were small things, but together they made a big difference in his hectic life and helped him to *maintain* . . . not always easy when one was chasing the American dream. This trip would be easy-peasy (Zac's term) and he'd be home before Alison and Zac even missed him.

The safety video finally concluded. "Beemo, ocean," Will commanded. The soothing sounds of a day at the beach filled the compartment, complete with images of lapping waves projecting onto the windows. It was Will's preferred driving ambience and one so real he could almost close his eyes and feel sun on his face. *All part of the Beemo experience.*

An uneventful ride to the airport, clear skies to Chicago, two days of blue-chip meetings, and dinner at Gibson's tonight—probably medium-rare filet mignon and a couple of cold Goose Island drafts.

It was, he thought, going to be a great day.

II.

D r. Stewart Wheeler pulled on his favorite Asics and walked out the front door, leaving it closed but unlocked. His legs felt good, limber, and he took a deep breath of California air. He began his run with long strides, counting the cadence of his soles and gaining energy from the spring of the pavement.

He loved these solitary early-morning hours before the Valley began to stir. Soon enough, he'd be knee-deep in calls and meetings. The fruit orchards he'd run through as a teenager were now sub-developments and strip malls—the cost of progress—and more people meant more noise and hassle. Running at five o'clock guaranteed that his exercise and meditation wouldn't be disturbed. This was *his* time, and he protected it fiercely.

As Chief Science Officer (CSO) for the Beemo Corporation, Stewart was head of a hundred-million dollar R&D group employing more than four-hundred scientists, researchers and engineers. His mission was simple: to ensure that Beemo remained at the forefront of the multi-billion-dollar autonomous driving industry. It was, Stewart had to admit, a dream job, but the pressure was constant, making his early-morning rituals critical to maintaining some balance of physical and mental stability, which was about as rare these days as a native Californian in the Valley.

Today he'd be listening to pitches from the founders of a dozen startups, all of them eager for a piece of the Beemo war chest. Like a Roman emperor, he sat in judgment, crushing dreams or bringing them to life with a wave of his hand. That kind of power was thrilling and, he had to admit, more than a little bit addictive. He knew that several startups were advancing cutting-edge technology that, if it worked as advertised, could further solidify Beemo's dominance in the ultracompetitive AV market and send its value through the roof. Given the recent IPO rumblings in the hallways, there was the potential of a life-changing event in his future. Happily (and fortuitously), he had opted to receive a larger share of stock options than most executives because he believed in the market and the technology, but above all, he believed in Jeff Beemer, Beemo's mercurial founder and CEO. Jeff was a genius and a visionary, and he'd recruited Stewart as Employee #6 into Beemo Corp. Together, they'd built the company into a juggernaut.

Not many people knew how far he'd come—from a five-room ranch house to graduating first in his class at Cal, a classic geek in glasses who spent his weekends studying instead of partying. The glasses were long gone (thanks to Lasik) and in a few short hours he would be deciding whether to invest tens of millions of dollars in some lucky founder's startup. He felt like Santa Claus on steroids, only he lived in a better climate, owned a Maserati, and controlled a budget that would have made the fat guy envious. Checking his watch and seeing that he'd completed his circuit faster than normal, Stewart decided to squeeze in one more mile.

It was, he thought, going to be a great day.

III.

Lieutenant Michael Finneran inspected the chamber of his service weapon before placing it in the holster, a ritual that his father had drilled into him from the first time they went hunting together. It was always safety first for the old man, Michael thought, and that sensibility allowed Declan Finneran to retire after a thirty-year police career and move to St. Augustine with his wife Maggie, where he now lived on a boat and did battle with sailfish instead of bad guys.

Michael had quite a way to go before retirement, but his career with the Boston Police Department was progressing nicely. He's been promoted to Lieutenant Detective after a few years in the Homicide Unit, and his lifelong friend Patrick Fitzgerald had just been elected mayor of Boston. "If I get this thing, Mikey," Pat told him, "I'll want people I trust around me. That means someone like you." Now that Pat had moved into his big new office in City Hall, Michael was scheduled to meet with him at eleven. The mayor-elect ran on a platform of bold ideas, and Michael couldn't wait to hear more about how those plans might include him. *Not bad for a couple of meatheads from Winthrop,* he thought.

Michael eased his Ford Crown Victoria into the northbound flow of traffic on Storrow Drive just as the sun began to break over the city. The department was phasing out the old Vics in favor of SUVs, but Michael remained a stubborn holdout. The Vic was solid; it *looked* like a cop car and, more important, it *felt* like a cop car. He'd keep the Vic as long as he could and if that made him a dinosaur in the department then so be it. Ahead of him, an egg-like Beemo taxicab veered across two lanes and into his path, almost cutting him off. *That's Boston for ya—even the robot cars are shit drivers.*

He checked the clock and guessed he'd be in the precinct early. This was a rarity and also good since he was behind on paperwork. His plan was to finish his reports by ten-thirty and jump the T to Government Center for his meeting with Pat. A central platform of the mayor-elect's campaign was combatting the influx of opiates and designer drugs that had crashed through Boston and other cities like a drug tsunami. That meant a task force headed by someone with the vision (and balls) to lead the charge. It would be a career opportunity for the right officer, not to mention a real chance to make a difference, a rarity on the force these days. It would also probably bring a certain amount of local celebrity. Pat had complimented Michael numerous times on his handling of that high-profile murder case in Beacon Hill last year. Balancing good police work with the deft touch required to deal with voracious local media was a high-wire act that had ruined many a promising career in Boston law enforcement, but Pat's vote of confidence could be exactly the boost Michael needed to steer his career in new directions.

A text popped up on his phone. Suzie. *C U tonite?*

Ignoring the Boston Police PSAs about the dangers of texting and driving, Michael tapped out a one-handed reply. *Of course.*

A few moments later: *Celebration?*

Michael chuckled. He had met Suzie three months ago at a Deep Purple concert at the Pavilion. Michael just happened to have the seat next to her, and clumsy jokes led to a smile, then a conversation, and then drinks at Whiskey Priest. Later that night, he'd lain awake, unable to sleep, staring at the ceiling and thinking about her. Declan told him this only happened with the special ones. Michael could kick in the door of a stash house or interrogate stone-cold killers but the thought of calling Suzie for a second date terrified him. When he finally built up the courage, she said yes. That was six dates ago.

Well see, he typed back with a characteristic indifference to spelling that she said made him even more endearing. Then, with an impulsive burst of bravado, he added a final flourish: ♥U

Suzie's reply came back almost immediately: *Me2*

Hope for the best and prepare for the worst was another big Declan-ism, but Michael allowed himself to feel a rising glow of optimism as he pulled the Vic into the garage and found a parking spot next to the elevator. In the always-bustling D-4 precinct, that almost never happened.

It was, he thought, going to be a great day.

IV.

Will busied himself by reviewing the folder of Zac's hospital bills that were coming due. Earlier that year, there'd been a health scare with Zac, but now everything was fine. Will had never felt more relieved.

He was counting on his Chicago deals to cover these expenses and maybe leave a little extra for a family vacation to Aruba. They deserved it, Alison said, after the year they'd had, and Will and Zac agreed. The past few months had been much better, almost back to normal.

Absorbed with numbers and forms, Will paid little attention to anything else until about twenty minutes into the ride when the car began to shake and then slow. The digital speedometer was ticking down, from 45 . . . to 38 . . . and then bottoming out at 20 as the car drifted into the bike lane. *What the hell*? he thought, turning around to look through the translucent back window for emergency lights or some other explanation. The Beemo hurked and jerked spasmodically, giving Will the impression that something was definitely wrong. His best guess was that the electric motor was either running low on juice or about to seize. *Shit, not today. Not when I have a flight.* Passing drivers veered around the wounded vehicle and expressed their empathy by leaning on their horns to deliver a sonic middle finger as the black egg teetered along the edge of the street.

Will generally found the Beemos to be reliable, but like all machines they were subject to the occasional hiccup. He'd broken down in a Beemo only once before, and knew from experience that the cars were programmed to follow strict protocols. First, it would scan for a safe location to pull over. At the time, his car had broken away from traffic and pulled off on a side road. Then, the car had informed him that it was experiencing mechanical difficulties and would contact Beemo Support on his behalf to request a replacement. Twenty minutes later, a new egg showed up and Will was on his way.

But today's circumstances were different. He was more time-crunched than usual and his flight to Chicago loomed large in his mind. They were making decent time but Will knew everything would change if he was forced to wait twenty or thirty minutes for another car.

"Beemo, why are we stopping?" he asked, irritation creeping into his voice.

"HELLO will butler," the car intoned, "WE'RE SORRY BUT . . . HELLO HELLO HELLO W-I-L-L B-U-T-L-E-Rrrrrrrrrr," the e-voice slurred drunkenly as the monitor and dashboard lights began flickering on and off before going completely dark. The car glided to a stop in the parking lane, its route display blank and the comfortable hum of the electric motor ceasing completely. No ocean sounds or waves gently lapping against the windows either. As far as Will could tell, they were dead in the water.

"Beemo, what's the problem?"

No response.

He tried again. "Beemo, status update."

Nothing.

Will's eyes dropped to the laminated placard below the display: *IN CASE OF EMERGENCY,* it read. He had looked past it so many times that its presence had barely registered. *Break glass in case of emergency,* he thought. *Everyone ignores the safety briefing until the plane is going down.* The letters were big and bold:

*YOUR BEEMO IS DESIGNED TO THE HIGHEST
SAFETY STANDARDS.
SHOULD AN ISSUE OCCUR,
PLEASE FOLLOW THESE STEPS:*

1. REMAIN CALM. STAY INSIDE THE VEHICLE.

2. ASK YOUR BEEMO TO DIAGNOSE AND FIX THE PROBLEM. IN MOST CASES, THE CAR WILL RE-PAIR ITSELF.

3. IF YOU NEED TO SPEAK WITH SOMEONE, CALL BEEMO SUPPORT ON THE INTERCOM OR DIAL DIRECT (888) 555-6600.

"Beemo, diagnose problem."

Silence.

"Beemo, call Support."

Nothing.

Will became more annoyed as he fumbled for his phone. Morning flights to Chicago were always full, and he'd need the luck of the Irish if he missed his plane and had to catch a later one. The back of his neck was growing warm, a sure sign that his blood pressure was beginning to rise, and he let loose with a string of profanities. A busy signal buzzed in his ear. *Other than the local sub shop, who the fuck has a busy signal in this day and age?*

He jabbed a finger to disconnect and redial. At that moment, the car's display flickered and then powered up. Something was different though; instead of displaying the normal route map, the screen was blood-red. Will stared at it, transfixed, until he saw text begin to scroll. It was the stark white font of a command prompt, meaning that some system somewhere wasn't working like it was supposed to.

VIRUS DETECTED.
LAUNCHING ZERO ANTIVIRUS . . .

The words shimmered on the screen and then dissolved into a series of bizarre characters that began flying in all directions, reminding Will of the *Matrix* screensaver Zac had installed on his Macbook. *Shit, this is all I need.* He drummed his fingers impatiently as he waited. *Who knows how goddamn long this is going to take?*

His third call to Beemo Support resulted in nothing more than the same busy signal droning with infuriating monotony. *Unbelievable.* Will flipped through his contacts until he found an old number for Boston Cab. Fully prepared to bail on his Beemo and grab another ride, he was poised to dial when the display blinked and reset again. Only this time, a different message blinked across the crimson screen:

ANTIVIRUS INITIALIZED. SYSTEM REBOOTING . . .
4 . . . 3 . . . 2 . . . 1 . . .

A low, primitive groan rose from the car's core and its systems vibrated back to life. "HELLLLLLLLO will butler," the robotic voice said, filling the chamber. "MY APOLOGIES FOR THE MINOR ISSUE BUT I'M NOW FULLY OPERATIONAL. LET'S GET ON THE ROAD AGAIN AND CONTINUE OUR TRIP TO logan airport." As if for emphasis, Willie Nelson's cheerful voice rang out over the speakers: "*On the road again, just can't wait to get on the road again . . . "* Pulling away from the curb, the Beemo picked up speed and maneuvered itself expertly back into the flow of traffic.

Relieved and a bit surprised to be on the move, Will checked his watch. *Only a ten-minute delay. I can live with that.* Except for the blood-dipped display and strange messages, the car appeared to be working fine. He was relieved they'd avoided the highways today; better to have a problem on Boylston Street than barreling down the highway at seventy-five miles an hour.

"Beemo, confirm destination and arrival time."

"will butler YOUR ETA IS NOW nine oh-nine. ENJOY THE RIDE WHILE BEEMO GETS YOU THERE BEAUTIFULLY, SAFELY AND ON TIME."

Satisfied, he tucked his laptop away in his briefcase and sat back in the leather seat. The lucent dome offered gorgeous views of the city. They were approaching Trinity Church where he and Alison occasionally attended Sunday services followed by brunch and Bloody Marys at Sonsie. The plaza buzzed with professionals, students and skateboarders. Will's eyes followed one ragged-looking boarder as he skimmed his deck along the curb, passing so close to the Beemo that Will could have practically reached out to high-five the dude. As he contemplated the poor souls stuck behind the wheels of their own cars, Will relished his own Beemo experience. So up-close and personal . . . so *present*. It made him feel like he was floating through the city in a giant bubble, like Glinda The Good Witch in *The Wizard of Oz*. Zac loved that movie.

Shotgun Willie finished his song and the Beemo was silent. The route map still hadn't reappeared, but when it did, he hoped it would still be pointing east towards the airport. Will was nervous that the lingering glitches could portend another time-wasting breakdown. A new message appeared and began to blink on screen:

REBOOT COMPLETE. VIRUS ID POSITIVE.
INITIATING KILL SEQUENCE . . .

Kill sequence? What the f^&' is that?* Obviously, there was still some sort of glitch in the car's systems. You could bet he'd be getting in touch with Beemo Customer Service and giving them an earful as soon as he landed in Chicago. He was a frequent rider, after all; they'd have to listen to him. Maybe if he was indignant enough they'd even throw some freebies his way, like the airlines did. It was worth a try.

The car was moving fast as they approached the red light at the intersection of Boylston and Berkeley. Still adrift in his thoughts, Will expected the Beemo to slow down. Instead, it began accelerating, the inertia pressing him back into his seat. The crosswalk bustled with people as the Beemo's speedometer crept up to 45 . . . 50 . . . then past 55 to 60.

Shit! We're going way too fast . . .

A young man in a blue hoodie stepped off the curb, staring at the phone in his hands and not bothering to check for approaching traffic. He had sandy hair and a matching goatee and a satchel slung over his shoulder . . . probably some kid on his way to work at Pinkberry, or the mailroom in Fidelity. *I bet he has Apple airpods in his ears too, cranked at full volume, oblivious—he doesn't even know we're coming.*

The Beemo wrenched hard left, cutting off a truck and putting itself on a direct course with Blue Hoodie. *What the fuck!?* Other pedestrians, catching sight of the speeding Beemo, jumped back, panicked, shouting a warning to Blue Hoodie. But everyone could only watch helplessly as the young man's fate raced toward him at sixty miles per hour.

In a split-second impact, the Beemo struck Blue Hoodie, passing through him like wet newspaper and flipping his body into then over the windshield. Shocked, Will swiveled to see Blue Hoodie's limp form land on the sidewalk with a dull thud, like a sand-filled scarecrow tossed off a building.

It killed him, Will thought crazily. *That boy must be dead and my car did it.* He felt an icy pit in his stomach and his head filled with a murky haze as he tried to process what had just happened. He knew the Beemo was programmed to stop in the event of an accident, but the car hadn't slowed at all. If anything, it was *energized*, gaining even *more* speed as it tore down Boylston Street with a vengeance.

Around them, startled bystanders stared in horror as a rising crescendo of screams pierced the air then grew faint as the evil egg sped on. Will sat rigid in his seat, eyes transfixed on the blood and jelly-like substance (*Brains?! Oh dear Christ!*) streaking across the windshield. He looked at the face staring back at him in the tinted glass, and he could barely recognize his own ashen reflection. In his forty-one years on Earth, Will Butler had only a passing familiarity with Death, but now he could feel its spidery fingers pulling at him. Then, like an icepick to the brain, he had a moment of pure clarity:

Maybe this is the day I die.

V.

The 911 call came in at eight-forty-nine from an hysterical BU student who had just seen her first dead body, motionless and bleeding, splayed out on the sidewalk in front of her. The emergency dispatch operator had a hard time understanding the girl, but did manage to make out "evilegg" and "ithinkhesdead" between wailing sobs.

This call was quickly followed by several more, and a clearer picture began to emerge of a hit-and-run accident at Boylston and Berkeley with at least one casualty. Alarmed, the operator notified her supervisor, who stepped in and immediately issued a citywide APB to Boston Police. Next, she placed a direct call to District D-4, the BPD station closest to the accident.

The supervisor's call was taken by Sergeant Kathleen Sullivan at D-4. She jotted notes on a pad as she listened, then hung up and walked briskly down the hall to Lieutenant Detective Michael Finneran's office. She could see him hunched over his computer, squinting at the screen, and regretted that she had to interrupt him with bad news. She rapped on the door to get his attention. "Lieutenant, we have a hit-and-run with a possible fatality at Boylston and Berkeley. Uniforms and EMTs are already en route. Witnesses say the vic was hit by a Beemo that just kept going. Suspect vehicle is still at large."

Michael thought back to the taxi that almost cut him off that morning. "You mean the robotaxi?" he asked. "I thought it was impossible for them to hurt people."

"I don't know, sir. All we have is that it was a Beemo and there's at least one victim. The Beemo is still unaccounted for."

Guess my meeting with Pat's going to have to wait. "What's that 10-20 again?"

"Boylston and Berkeley."

His brow wrinkled. "That's a busy area, pedestrians everywhere. Did we get a plate number or know where it's headed?"

"Negative on the plate. Witnesses say the car was traveling eastbound on Boylston toward the Common, but you know that area. Lots of side streets, it could turn off anywhere."

Michael stood and approached the map of Boston tacked to his wall. Usually he didn't need it; he carried a detailed map of the city in his head. "It's still the morning rush so traffic will slow it down. Let's think about this . . . the first big intersection is Boylston and Charles. Get someone there. Also, send units to cover the bridges . . . if the car keeps heading east it'll hit the water. Tell everyone to keep eyes out for a Beemo that's speeding or driving erratically."

Racing to keep up, Sergeant Sullivan wrote furiously in her notebook. Michael rubbed his forehead like the solution lay just beneath his skin and could be massaged out. *What am I missing?* "Christ, there must be hundreds of those black eggs in the city. We're going to need some luck finding it." Pulling on his jacket, he was heading for the door when he stopped, a strange look crossing his face. "How do you stop a car without a driver?" he asked. Sergeant Sullivan, still busy scribbling notes, looked up at Michael and shook her head.

This is really bad. A robot car that's already hit one person running amok in downtown Boston. "We're going to need spike strips, as many as we can find. Also, get me somebody from Beemo on the phone. *They* built this goddamn Frankenstein—*they* must know how to stop it."

"Yes, sir."

"I'll be mobile until the suspect's located and we can pick up pursuit. I'm going to the accident scene now to see if we can learn anything useful from witnesses. Notify me the second we make a positive ID and know the perp's 10-20. Oh, and one more thing, Sergeant: call the mayor's office and tell him I can't make our meeting." His head buzzing, Michael hurried toward the bank of elevators, stunned by how quickly his amazing day was turning to shit.

VI.

Although their taxis were designed to be fully-autonomous self-driving machines, the Beemo design team had acknowledged that there may be certain instances in which human intervention might be needed to stop one of their cars. Accidents. Malfunctions. Medical emergencies. That sort of thing.

The team, raised on pop culture icons like *The Terminator* and Asimov's *Three Laws of Robotics*, had insisted on installing fail-safe measures to allow people to assert control over the machines. There had been a lengthy and impassioned debate over whether to include steering wheels and brake pedals for passenger use, with advocates on both sides pleading their cases. But in the end, Stewart made the executive decision not to include either safety feature. Instead, the primary fail-safe was a red four-inch STOP button that stuck out like a sprinkler head from the ceiling, allowing the passenger to bring the car to a stop in the event of an emergency.

Affectionately referred to by Beemo's designers as "the dead man's switch," pressing this oversized STOP button initiated a series of actions. First, the Beemo would slow down and scan its immediate environment for a safe place to pull over. Second, it would unlock and open both doors to allow the passenger to exit. Finally, it would transmit an alert to the Beemo Corporation indicating that one of its passengers had just overridden the drive system and stopped their car. This alert would be picked up by a tech at the nearest Support Center, who would then initiate contact with the passenger to assess the situation and work out the best course of action.

At this point, all Will could think about was stopping the car and getting the hell away from it. It went without saying that he'd never ride in another damn Beemo as long as he lived, but for now he just wanted out. *I need to go back and check on Blue Hoodie. Maybe he's OK?* Without considering the consequences, Will reached up, flipped open the protective lid, and slammed his palm against the STOP button.

Nothing happened.

Desperate, he hit the button a second time, unwilling to believe it was inoperable. Nothing again. He pounded at it anyway, his hand stinging with the force. Suddenly, he heard a click. His seat belt harness had released, pitching him forward to the floor. Confused, he was scrambling back up when the car wrenched violently to the right and sent him flying across the compartment. He impacted hard into the full-length window and would have been knocked unconscious had his arms not gone up reflexively to protect his head.

Dazed, Will struggled to focus. His right shoulder flamed with a pain that made him think it might be broken. Before he could react, the car swung hard left, sending him tumbling in the opposite direction. Flailing out, his hands found a metal support pole and he clung to it grimly as the Beemo continued to snake back and forth in violent, unpredictable spasms, like a mechanical bull trying to throw its rider.

An insane idea suddenly popped into his head: *it's trying to hurt me. That's why the seat belt opened. The car did it. It's trying to hurt or maybe even kill me.* A wave of despair washed over him and he squeezed his eyes shut. Will considered himself more spiritual than religious, and he hadn't really prayed since Zac was ill, but he prayed now, the words spilling out in a babbling stream that promised any-thing—or everything—if God would only step in and save him.

He felt the Beemo slow and there was a moment of disbelief—*divine intervention?* until he saw it was the traffic that had forced the car to cease its furious gyrations. Bruised and in pain, Will pulled himself off the floor and collapsed into a seat, snapping the seat belt tight. *Not that it mattered if the egg decides to take another shot at me. Jesus, I'm in trouble. Nasty big giant fucking trouble.*

The Beemo had already killed one person and Will couldn't help thinking he'd be the next. The seat belt incident proved one thing: even as a *rider*, the car could get to him. Thirty minutes ago he was reclined and comfortable, marveling at the Beemo experience. Now, he realized with horror, he was a hostage. The car was taking him along for the ride whether he liked it or not, and he'd have a three-hundred-and-sixty degree view of whatever carnage the Beemo was prepared to mete out. If it didn't kill him first.

Grasping the support pole tightly and bracing himself for whatever might come next, Will tried mightily to ignore the dark voices in the back of his head whispering that there was no way this day would end well for him.

VII.

The Support Technician at Beemo's northeast office had just settled into her workspace with a cheese danish and steaming mug of black tea when the message flashed across her terminal screen:

ALERT: Vehicle ID#79058 STOPPED by passenger
WILL BUTLER (AA 576930)
LOCATION: Boston MA
<LAT> 42°21'30" N <LNG> 71°03'35" W
Run vehicle diagnostics (Y/N)?

So much for a quiet morning, she thought, keying 'Y' to initiate a full system scan. With fifty-six thousand vehicles operating across eighteen major cities, she'd seen this scenario many times before. Actual mechanical problems were less likely than passengers behaving badly and wanting to see what happened when they pressed the STOP button. Alcohol was usually a factor, and Beemo had revoked the riding privileges of several passengers who just couldn't get that big red button out of their buzzed brains and resist the temptation to give it a smack.

Her scan results came back quickly:

Mechanical: OK - Electrical: OK - Comm: OK – External: OK.

Initiate vehicle contact (Y/N)?

Pulling on her headset, the tech placed a call through to the car's intercom and called up the passenger profile on her terminal. *Will Butler.* He was Gold status; a frequent Beemo traveler and not normally the type to take gratuitous swipes at the red button. The smile in his photograph was coy, like Will Butler knew a secret that nobody else knew. *Howdy, Will,* she thought. *It's a little early for imbibing, so let's see what's going on with you.*

Expecting to hear the chime of a successful connection, she was greeted instead by a series of clicks and hissing in her ears. "Hello? Mr. Butler?" she raised her voice above the static. "This is Alyssa with Beemo Support. Can you hear me?"

Just more clicks and buzzing and then dead air. No more sounds, no connection to the car. Nothing at all.

Alyssa clicked to disconnect and redial. Her second attempt yielded nothing more than a low-level hiss that suddenly amplified into an otherworldly shriek that lanced through her ears. Reflexively, she jerked her head backward, sending the headset flying and breaking the harsh tone. *What the f&°*# was that??*

Falling back on procedure, Alyssa located Will Butler's cell phone number to call him directly. Glaring at her headset, which still lay limp on the carpet, she powered up her speakerphone instead. Her ears still rang from the noise, and Alyssa had to admit it unnerved her a little bit. *More mechanical than human, but . . . eerie. Like a scream from outer space.* This time her call went through, the line ringing one . . . two . . . three . . . four . . . five times before someone finally picked up. The voice was muffled: "Hello?"

There you are, Will Butler. "Mr. Butler? This is Alyssa with Beemo Support. Can you hear me?"

There was a pause. "It's all static, it just hit . . . "

"Mr. Butler, it's Alyssa with Beemo Support. I'm calling because . . . "

Will cut her off, the panicked rush of his words making her blood run cold. "The car just hit someone. He was wearing a blue hoodie and I think he's dead but I don't know for sure but probably. We hit him *hard*. I tried to stop it. The button's not working and I kept pressing it but it's not working then my seat belt opened and the car started swerving like it *knew* I was trying to get out and wanted to stop me." Will, out of breath, stopped talking.

Alyssa couldn't believe what she was hearing. "Did you just say your Beemo hit a pedestrian?"

"Yes, a guy walking across Boylston street in a blue hoodie . . . it hit him and kept going. Why isn't it stopping, why can't we stop? I have to get out of here and check on him."

She paused for a moment, protocol demanding that she verify what she had just heard. "Mr. Butler, don't take this the wrong way, but what you're saying is incredibly serious. How do I know you're telling me the truth?"

Will practically spat through the receiver. "Do you think I would bullshit about something like this? I'm fucking Gold with Beemo, I use you all the damn time. I'm telling you, *the car hit someone and it won't stop or let me out.* The cops must know by now—there were witnesses everywhere. I keep pressing the goddamn button to stop it, but nothing's happening."

If he's telling the truth, I have to escalate. NOW. "Mr. Butler, listen to me. I need you to call 911 and report what you just told me. The call needs to come directly from you so the police can trace your phone and location. Can you do that?"

"Yeah."

"I'm going to initiate an override and take control of your car. I'll pull it over and let you out so you can get to a safe place. Agreed?"

"I hope this works because the systems are all screwed up. The screen is red and weird messages keep popping up."

What's he talking about? Alyssa struggled to keep calm and focused. "I've got your back, Will, and I'm going to get you through this. You dial 911 and I'll do my part. When I know you're safe, I'll call you back, OK?"

"You better hurry. We're going fifty down a street full of people. I'm afraid something bad is going to happen."

"We'll get through this together. I'm hanging up now so you can call 911. Good luck." Alyssa terminated the call and immediately typed an override sequence into the vehicle's control panel that would let her take control of the car. While she had trained for this procedure, she had never actually executed it for real. *I can't believe I have to do this now.* Swallowing hard, she brought up the car's onboard cameras, which provided multiple views of its environment in every direction. *Christ they're going fast,* she thought, gawking as grainy images rushed by in a blur. Maximizing the front camera into a full-screen view of the road ahead, her picture was obscured by something dark and irregular running across the lens. *Like they ran through a mud puddle, but thicker. Darker.*

Alyssa recoiled in horror as she fully understood what she was looking at. *That's blood. Oh God, there's blood on the camera!* The severity of the situation hit her hard. Her hands shook as she gripped the joystick and prepared to remotely steer the speeding three-ton machine off the road with limited visibility and only a blood-smeared camera to guide her. A message flashed across the screen:

Initiate manual override? (Y/N)

Alyssa pressed 'Y' and steeled herself to the task. The stakes were too high to fail. *I didn't sign up for this shit.* Doubts crept into her mind and she wished she were anywhere but here right now. *How am I ever going to do this?* The system response came back in seconds:

Manual override REJECTED. Unknown error code (79).

WTF?! She'd been around long enough to know most of the typical error codes—dead battery, system malfunction, maintenance required—but code 79 was a new one. Panicked, her heart pounding, she carefully re-entered the sequence and held her breath.

Manual override REJECTED. Unknown error code (79).

Alyssa felt sick as she turned away from her terminal. *The sky is falling.* Grabbing her personal cell phone, she found the number she'd never had to dial before that would connect her to Emergency Services at Beemo headquarters in Cupertino. For a Beemo support tech, it was the equivalent of hitting the panic button.

As she dialed, Alyssa couldn't get Will Butler's coy smile out of her head. She wondered if he'd ever flash that secret smile again. Will was in serious danger. She'd taken her one shot and missed. *I told him I had his back, but I lied.* It was now up to someone else to save his ass.

When her call connected, Alyssa began an urgent recitation of everything she could recall to the voice on the other end of the line. After she hung up, she offered up a silent prayer for Will Butler. He'd need all the help he could get.

VIII.

Returning from his run, Stewart could hear his cell phone ringing just as he opened the front door. *And so the day begins*, he thought, kicking off his Asics and glancing down at the screen.

It was Matthew Palmer, Beemo's Chief Operating Officer. It was unusual for Matthew to be calling him so early and at home. Briefly, he considered ignoring the call, but the breach in protocol intrigued him. *Something's up.* Sliding his fingers through his thick grey hair, Stewart took a deep breath and answered. "Matthew. Good morning."

Matthew didn't bother with formalities. "Stewart, we have a situation. One of our cars is running out of control in Boston and it hit a pedestrian. The passenger can't stop the car and the override sequence isn't working. I need your help."

Stewart went cold. "Boston?"

"Yes."

Oh shit. "Does Jeff know?"

"Not yet. He's on the final day of a five-day silent retreat in Telluride. You know what those are like—no phone, no computer, no nothing. He's pretty much unreachable until he comes down from the mountain. The only thing we *can* do is call Anna at the ranch and have her drive up there, but I'm reluctant to make that call unless we have to."

Shit—the timing couldn't be worse. Twice a year, Beemo's eccentric CEO immersed himself in a silent retreat, detoxing from all technology and spending his days meditating, exercising, and reading. Even in a crisis—and this certainly seemed to qualify—stepping into Jeff's solitude could bring repercussions. Stewart didn't blame Matthew for hesitating, and he also agreed that handling things themselves was the better option.

Stewart put the COO on speaker and walked rapidly across the foyer into his office and flipped open his laptop. "What's the vehicle ID?"

"79058."

Stewart typed the ID in and stared intently as data scrolled across the screen. "I can see the point of failure here . . . it doesn't look systemic. The issue's probably localized to the car itself. Any other problems in Boston?"

"No . . . I mean, not yet. Not that we know of."

"The dead man's switch can malfunction but a remote override should work. I'll try it as an admin." Stewart's fingers flew as he entered a long string of commands and hit ENTER. The response was immediate: *Administrative override REJECTED. Unknown error code (79).*

Unlike Alyssa in Tech Support, Stewart knew what error code 79 really meant: one of the car's primary systems had overridden all the other systems and seized control. *Not good.* "Negative on the admin override. One more thing to try . . . " His brow darkened with concentration. "The backdoor. Once I'm in I can disable the drive function." Backdoors were a programming trick Stewart had used ever since he'd written his first lines of Pascal; it enabled him to bypass the usual security protocols and gain direct access to the car's main CPU. He entered the master password and was shocked to read the system response: *Password incorrect; access denied.* He typed it in again. Same result.

That's impossible. Only a couple of people have the master password and they'd never change it without notifying me. "Damn it, the backdoor's not working either. I need my office workstation. Where are you?"

"I'm in the first floor conference room and Sophie Chin's on her way in too." Sophie was Beemo's tough-as-nails general counsel and her involvement meant that Matthew was already thinking about damage control. A muffled female voice spoke in the background and Stewart guessed it was Melissa Dunbar, Matthew's assistant. "Mel's trying to reach the passenger on his cell but no luck yet. I need you in here *now*, Stewart. And one more thing—don't breathe a word of this to anyone. Got it?"

"Of course."

"I have a bad feeling about this," Matthew said before hanging up. Stewart sat back in his chair and stared out the window, worry lines creasing his otherwise handsome face. *A face with character*, his grandmother used to say. He was glad she wasn't here to see the coming storm.

Stewart dialed Srini Kasam, his handpicked #2 in R&D, and one of the only Beemo people he trusted implicitly. Despite the early hour, Srini picked up right away. "Hello, Stewart."

"Srini, we have a problem. It's Boston. One of the Zeros hit a pedestrian and it's blowing through all of the safeguards: the dead man's switch, manual override and even the backdoor. Nothing's working. Did you change the master password?"

"Not without telling you. No way."

"That's what I thought. I think the car's in self-protection mode and it's actively working to keep us out. It's black hat time, Srini; I need you to hack in and shut it down. Torch the CPU if you have to but the Zero needs to be stopped. I'm on my way to the War Room at HQ right now and just texted you the vehicle ID. Keep this conversation to yourself and call me the minute you have something."

"I'm on it," Srini said, and Stewart could hear Srini's fingers racing across the keyboard before he had even hung up. Srini was beyond competent; if he couldn't figure it out, nobody could. Stewart had plucked him from the tree at CalPoly, a fresh-faced engineer with immense talents that Stewart recognized immediately. He had put Srini to work on the Advanced Concepts team and nine months later he was leading it. The man had proven himself many times over, but Stewart also knew that his protégé had a darker side, a penchant for hacking that had gotten him into trouble in the past. At Stewart's urging, however, Srini became part of the system instead of burning it down, yet there *were* times when Stewart found it expedient to let the lion out of the cage. This was definitely one of those times. He was sure Srini could penetrate the car's defenses, but how much damage it would cause before then was the billion-dollar question. Not million, *billion*.

Dead bodies in Boston.

Christ Almighty.

Stewart glanced at his watch. *One more thing to do.* Launching a custom browser designed to handle highly secure and anonymous transactions, he typed an address that connected him to a hard drive he'd set up in the most remote corner of the dark web. Selecting several files, he began copying these to a series of remote servers. One server resided in his sister's house in Adelaide and the other sat behind a secure firewall in the law offices of Brown, Beranek & Newman in San Francisco. When the transfers were complete, Stewart folded the laptop into a bag and dropped it by the front door. He wouldn't have time to shower, so instead he threw on a pair of jeans, a black t-shirt and the first sport coat within reach. Passable, he collected his bag and walked outside, locking the door behind him.

If today was the day when the music stopped, Stewart Wheeler would make damn sure he wasn't the only one left standing without a chair.

IX.

Will felt rigid as marble after hanging up with the Beemo tech. A storm raged in his head. He knew he had to dial 911, but his arms weren't cooperating.

He thought about Blue Hoodie, who had just been walking on his way to work or someplace else when the speeding car came out of nowhere and instantly erased the rest of his life. That young man was a memory now. *There's no way he could have survived; there's pieces of him on the windshield.* The senselessness of his brutal death shook Will to the core. The more he thought about it, the more his anger grew until it provided the spark that broke his paralysis. Placing the phone on speaker, Will punched in 9-1-1.

"911 operator. What's your emergency?"

"My name is Will Butler and the car I'm riding in just hit a pedestrian. I don't know what to do."

There was a brief pause. Will could hear her breathe. "Sir, you say the car you're riding in hit someone? Who's driving?"

"There *is* no driver. It's a Beemo . . . an evil egg . . . self-driving taxi, you know? It picked me up in Belmont to take me to Logan and then ran over someone in the crosswalk. Beemo called me and they know and they're supposed to stop it but we're still moving."

"Okay, Will, I'm with you." The operator was well-trained, addressing him by name with a cool, even voice to keep him calm as well. "I need you to tell me where you are *right now*."

Will strained to catch sight of a street sign or landmark he recognized. Naturally, Boston placed the tiniest possible street markers in the least visible spots imaginable—when they marked the streets at all, that is. "I'm on Boylston. I can see the Four Seasons on my right."

"Okay Will, officers are on their way to you right now. Are you in immediate danger?"

"Yes," he hissed. "I just *told* you. I'm in a Beemo taxi that hit someone. There *is* no driver! I can't stop it. It's fucking out of control. I *am* in danger."

"Will, I need . . . et . . . a . . . em . . . den . . . cee . . . " The operator's voice descended into a jumble of static before a metallic screech burned through the air. *Shit that's awful.* Cringing, he dropped his phone to the floor to cover his ears. The shrieking continued. "Hello, hello?!" he shouted. Suddenly, silence and an error message: *Call failed.*

MotherF&%#*$.* Will reached down to retrieve his phone when, without warning, the sound system flipped on, filling the compartment with Guns N' Roses at maximum volume:

WELCOME TO THE JUNGLE, WE'VE GOT FUN 'N' GAMES

. . .

To enhance the passenger experience, Beemo had (of course) invested in a top-of-the-line sound system, and at top volume the noise was overpowering, like sticking your head into a 747 engine. Will covered his ears again as he felt the cab pulse with noise, every note a sledgehammer blow to his skull:

SHA NA NA NA NA NA KNEES . . . KNEES . . .

As if the sonic assault wasn't bad enough, they'd maneuvered onto a clear stretch of road and the taxi began swerving again. His seat belt held this time but every jarring turn sent shockwaves through his body. His phone wasn't so lucky; it slid off the seat and flew through the air, smashing against the window and landing face up on the floor, its screen a spider web of cracks. *Fuck me.* Will suddenly felt very much alone. *That was my lifeline to the world.*

Like an errant missile, the Beemo sped ahead, plowing through traffic while Will desperately held on, his eyes fixed on the blurred landscape to prepare for the next danger. They were closing fast on an intersection paralyzed by a logjam of cars stretching in all directions, and he hoped that would force the Beemo to stop. Instead, the taxi swung hard left, crossing the median and bisecting two lanes of on-coming traffic before striking the curb with teeth-shattering force. The impact sent the taxi briefly airborne before it landed on the sidewalk and skidded into an empty bus shelter, obliterating the lean-to in an explosion of flying glass and metal.

Barely slowing, the Beemo straightened its course on the sidewalk and accelerated toward a crowd of pedestrians, most of whom had turned to see the source of the commotion. They stood frozen in place as the black egg rapidly closed the distance between them . . . a bionic predator steaming into a herd of gazelle with murderous intent.

X.

When Michael Finneran arrived at the first accident scene, the blanket over the prone figure told him all he needed to know before he even saw the attending EMT's expression. *Vehicular homicide.*

The uniforms on site had already cordoned off the area with yellow crime tape and a crowd of onlookers bunched along the perimeter, morbidly curious. Away from the crowd, several BPD officers were speaking with a small group. He could see Chet Bradley, a friend and veteran officer, talking quietly with a young woman in a BU sweatshirt. Her tear-stained face told Michael that she was probably a witness.

"Hi, Chet."

"Lieutenant," Officer Bradley replied, addressing him formally. "This is Meilin Han. She saw the accident. Meilin, this is Lieutenant Finneran. He's the officer in charge of this investigation."

Poor girl, Michael thought, recognizing the same look of shock he'd seen so many times in a career dealing with people who had experienced very bad things. He spoke gently. "Ms. Han, I'm Michael. I know this is hard for you, so thank you for your help. I'm here to make sure nobody else gets hurt. Can you tell me what you saw?"

Meilin sniffled and took a deep breath. She spoke with an accent. "The man was crossing the street and the car hit him. It didn't even stop. He was walking right in front of me and I tried to help him but his head was bleeding and he wasn't breathing . . . I tried to help but he wha . . . wha . . . was . . . gone." Her voice hitched and she began to sob again.

"I'm sorry, Ms. Han. I know this is difficult. Was it a Beemo?"

"Yes . . . an evil egg. Shiny, black . . . like the others."

"Did you see where it went after . . . " Michael trailed off, catching himself. No need to state the obvious.

Meilin pointed up Boylston Street. "That way."

An officer Michael didn't know approached them. "Lieutenant Finneran? Sorry to bother you, but there's a call for you from dispatch."

Michael reached out to squeeze Meilin's shoulder and give her his most reassuring look. "Thank you, Ms. Han. You've been a big help. Believe it or not, you'll get through this. Officer Bradley needs to ask you a few more questions and then he'll make sure you get home." Meilin looked at him through tear-reddened eyes and nodded. *Brave girl.*

The uniform led Michael to his squad car and handed him the radio mic. "Finneran."

Sergeant Sullivan's voice crackled through the loudspeaker. "Lieutenant, an emergency operator just spoke with the passenger in our suspect vehicle. Passenger's name is Will Butler. The car's northbound on Boylston and they just passed the Four Seasons. We have a couple of units close by and they're en route now."

Each step closer and closer. "You said northbound on Boylston by the Common?"

"Yes sir."

"That's a straight line to the State House," Michael said. *This can't be terrorism, can it? What if a terrorist took control of the taxi and packed it full of explosives and now they're going to drive it right into the heart of state government?* "Any indication they might be targeting the gold dome?"

"It's hard to say at this point, sir, but we've taken the precaution of alerting Capitol Police and closing off a two-block perimeter. Nobody gets in or out." The politicians would probably squawk, but Michael could live with that. Better to be cautious and apologize later than allow a major incident to happen on his watch.

"Well done. I'm headed in that direction now. Tell all units to use channel six for updates on our suspect. Copy?"

"Roger that, Lieutenant. I'll put out the word."

"What's the story with the Beemo people? Any luck?"

"Not yet, sir, but I'll get through to them."

"I know you will. Patch them through as soon as you connect. We could really use their help. Headed to Boylston now. Over and out."

Michael strode back to the Vic, climbed inside and drove off. Maneuvering past the crime scene, he flipped on his lights and siren to clear a path. Having seen the Beemo's chaos firsthand, he steeled himself for what lay ahead. Something was telling him that it would be bad. *Very* bad.

XI.

Thirty minutes after hanging up with Matthew, Stewart's transport pulled up to Beemo HQ. Like all Beemo executives, he had unlimited access to the company's fleet of vehicles and he worked on his laptop while the car drove.

He hadn't broken the problem yet, but he was getting a clearer picture of what was happening. What he needed was uninterrupted time. He wished like hell he could sneak through a rear door, but Jeff insisted that every Beemo employee come and go through a single entrance point. *Creative collisioning,* he called it. In theory, it was designed to encourage random encounters that would then lead to greater collaboration and "out-of-the-box" thinking. To Stewart, it sounded more like dime-store bullshit from the lizard-like consultants slinking around the building, but he'd never tell Jeff that. At least most of his co-workers wouldn't arrive for another hour or so.

Entering the lobby, he waved to the desk crew and they waved back. *That's good,* he thought. No signs of panic, no looks of undue consternation. *It means our problem is still contained and hasn't leaked yet.* Given the early hour, the building was still dark and Stewart's motion through the hallway left a trail of lights to his office. He picked up his workstation and headed back down the lit corridor to the War Room.

The conference room doors were locked from the inside, and Stewart could hear voices that suddenly went quiet after he knocked. "Who's there?" Matthew called out.

"It's Stewart, Matthew."

The handle clicked and Matthew appeared, his face serious. "Come in, Stewart," he said, locking the doors behind him. Sophie Chin was already seated at the oversized table. She gave him a terse nod. Matthew's assistant Melissa stood in the corner by a window, murmuring into her phone. Stewart took a seat at the table, opened his workstation and glanced down at his phone. *Nothing from Srini.*

As was his style, Matthew took charge. "Now that Stewart's here, let's review what we know. We know that one of our cars hit a pedestrian. No info yet on the victim's status but we need to plan for all possibilities. When there've been accidents before involving people, the cars shut themselves down and we were able to limit the damage. But in this case there's some sort of malfunction that's crippling our controls. There's a passenger too, a . . . uh . . . " Matthew glanced down at his notes. " . . . Will Butler, who repeatedly pressed the dead man's switch but appears unable to stop or exit the vehicle. We've made multiple attempts to access the car's systems but they've all failed. We can't control the vehicle and have no apparent means to stop it. Stewart, any progress on your side?" Stewart shook his head.

"Failure . . . after . . . failure." Matthew intoned, pausing to let the words sink in as he looked around the room. His growing anger was evidenced by a Y-shaped vein beginning to throb in his forehead, a familiar sight in meetings. "As far as I can tell, this leaves us smack dab in the middle of a giant shitshow with no ability to stop one of our cars from injuring or killing more people, not to mention the worst PR disaster this company has ever seen and may not survive."

Other than Melissa's hushed conversation in the corner, the room was silent. Sophie spoke first, and when she began Stewart knew exactly where this conversation was headed.

"Stewart, how could this happen? You're in charge of the fleet. Nothing goes on the road without your OK. We're not here to assign blame . . . but how could one of our cars just go rogue like this?"

Fuck you, Sophie. Typical lawyer already pointing her lawyer's finger. At me. "In the forty-five minutes since Matthew alerted me, that's exactly what I'm trying to figure out." He and Sophia had clashed before, and Stewart took a measure of satisfaction in mansplaining his response to her. "You know we're sailing off the edge of the map in Boston. You were in the room when Jeff made the announcement. The entire leadership team supported the decision, including you, Sophie. Both of you, in fact."

Sophie's eyes flashed dark. "I knew we were testing prototypes in Boston, but I had no idea it was this risky. We went along because it was what Jeff wanted, but none of us really knew what you two were working on. We trusted *your* judgment and now you've unleashed a homicidal car on the public." While Sophie's words were overwrought, they weren't entirely wrong, and her underlying message was unmistakable: *somebody's going to take the fall for this, and you're at the top of my list.*

Before Stewart could respond, Matthew held up his hand. "Accusations aren't going to get us anywhere. We need solutions. Stewart, I didn't press you or Jeff for more details about Boston and that was a mistake. But all bets are off now. I need to know exactly what we're dealing with."

Stewart demurred. "You didn't know because Jeff instructed me to keep our work confidential. Strictly on a need-to-know basis." He paused and then continued. "At the time, you didn't need to know."

Matthew exploded. "I'd say we pretty much *need to fucking know*! We're talking life and death here, not some bullshit office politics. What exactly *did* you put under the hood of those cars, Stewart?"

Stewart sensed the other execs aligning against him, and he weighed the potential costs of holding out. While Matthew was not technically his boss, he *was* nominally in charge during Jeff's absence. Resisting him could bring blowback, especially in a crisis. The urgency of the situation forced his hand and pushed him to a decision.

"I'll show you," he said, then busied himself with his workstation. The lights dimmed as Stewart projected a 3D vehicle schematic onto the massive conference room screen.

"My team and I have been working on a new model for over a year. A 100% self-sufficient vehicle that runs and repairs itself. Officially it's the 5200, but we call it the "Zero" because it requires zero human in-tervention. It's really the perfect AV and its business model is flawless: a self-driving car that requires no overhead and is always on the clock. To get there, we've been experimenting with advanced AI that we acquired from our partners. Really mind-blowing stuff. Completely next-gen intelligence that blows away everything we'd seen before. So good, in fact, that we'd destroy the competition and take over the market within seven to nine months. That's months . . . not years. Beemo's value would skyrocket and we'd all get rich. But there were . . . problems."

Stewart paused to pour himself a glass of water. His audience was rapt, their attention fixed on him. He took a long swig and swallowed. "Viruses. The code was so advanced that it became unstable and highly susceptible to malicious viruses. This threatened to torpedo the whole project but Jeff promised whatever funding we needed to get it right. He knew its potential. We hired an army of programmers to develop an antivirus capability that would make the car impregnable to viruses and malicious attacks. It was hard as hell but we finally got it right. The Zero became a highly-intelligent, virus-killing machine that could adapt to mutations on the fly and, even better, share its learnings with every car in the fleet. When a Zero encounters a virus, it figures out how to kill it and then transmits this knowledge to all the other Zeros. In this way, we create a self-determined ecosystem that over time becomes invulnerable to attack. We'd found the perfect balance between AI and antivirus, and for a time it solved our problems."

Stewart continued. "With all the money we spent, there was immense pressure to show results. We demonstrated the prototype to Jeff and he went crazy. We all know Jeff's a visionary, and he saw Zeros as the ultimate disrupter that would lead to a glorious AV revolution with Beemo at the vanguard. He pushed us to begin testing in live markets right away, but I told him we weren't ready. We'd fixed the first big problem but we'd run into another. Something we didn't anticipate."

Matthew leaned in. "What was it?"

"You need to realize that AI isn't a finite product but an evolution. Machine intelligence can mutate in unexpected ways and not all of them can be controlled. Specifically, the Zero was exhibiting signs of what's called convergent behavior. The cars would pursue their objectives with such single-minded purpose that they could act harmfully, like driving across a crowded sidewalks to meet on-time arrival goals. The Zero would achieve its objective, sure, but at a cost that was unacceptably high." Stewart replaced the schematic on the screen with a video panel. "Watch this."

The group was suddenly transported into the front grill of a Zero heading straight toward a brick wall at high speed. Everyone gasped as the car made impact, killing the picture in a burst of static. "That's camera footage from a Zero prototype that elected to smash itself into a building to kill an infecting virus. We'd made antivirus so powerful that its primary directive—killing the virus—overrode *all other* systems and directed the car to destroy itself, thus destroying the virus. *That's* convergent behavior. The car's systems were becoming smarter and evolving in ways we didn't understand. Achieving a balance between two experimental and unstable agents was fragile at best, and at worst, it was metastasizing into something beyond our control."

"We walked that tightrope for months until a new infusion of funds from Jeff brought us to a point where I could support a trial launch of ten vehicles in a highly-controlled test environment. But Jeff wasn't going to let anything interfere with his vision. He insisted we pick the first market and activate a fleet of Zeros right away. It was an impossible decision but it had to be made, so we chose Boston. We already have a fleet of standard cars active there, so the Zeros blended in perfectly. We've been running thirty Zeros in Boston for two months now and they were outperforming all expectations . . . until today."

Stewart reached for his water glass again. He'd never felt so thirsty in his life. The executives were silent, struggling to wrap their heads around the bombshell he'd just dropped. Outside, faint sounds of incoming Beemos carrying the day's first employees could be heard, all of them blissfully unaware of the shitstorm awaiting them.

Matthew spoke first. "*Thirty*? There are thirty more of these Zeros in Boston? I had no idea we deployed live without having full confidence in the safety and integrity of all of our vehicles. You're telling me now that the core systems of these cars are fundamentally unstable? How could you or Jeff or anyone else on the team not see something like this coming?"

Stewart looked Matthew squarely in the eyes. "Jeff wanted the Zeros in the market, so we did it. It's that simple."

Matthew was incredulous. "You knew the risks, Stewart. You could have resigned. Christ, you could have gone public. Instead, you became part of the problem by giving in to Jeff's worst instincts, and now we're all paying the price." The Y-vein vibrated on his forehead. "If I didn't need you right now, Stewart, I'd have Security escort you out. But I *do* need you. We're in the middle of a crisis and you have more knowledge about this car than anyone else. I need every option out on the table. So, tell me, what the hell are we going to do about it?"

Stewart closed his workstation, killing the video feed. "The usual shutdown protocols aren't going to work, so let's not waste our time. The Zero knows we're trying to damage it and it's entered into a kind of self-preservation mode. We can't even contact the passenger because the car's deliberately sabotaging all comms. The assumption moving forward needs to be that the Zero will do whatever is necessary to defend itself from outside threats, including us. What's working to our benefit is that we designed it and we know its vulnerabilities. I've got Srini hacking his way in right now, and once he does, he'll swing a wrecking ball through its systems."

"How long will it take?" Matthew asked. "What if it takes him an hour. Or two? An uncontrollable steel-reinforced AV can cause massive damage in an hour. What then?"

"Then we have one final option: we go nuclear and broadcast a kill signal to every car in the northeast corridor. We shut them all down. Fifteen thousand vehicles, all dead in a nanosecond."

Matthew was incredulous. "There are only thirty Zeros running, right? Why don't we just kill those thirty?"

"We can't do a pinpoint strike because the Zeros run on the same network as all our other cars. We had to use the infrastructure we already have, and the kill signal is designed to protect the *entire* network from a major hack or a terrorist attack. It can't target individual cars. That's thing one. *Thing two* is the revenue loss and PR hit we'd take, which would probably cripple us just as we're going mainstream. *Thing three*—and this is a biggie—is that we need the nuclear codes to execute and there's only one person with those codes, and right now he's on the mountaintop seeking enlightenment and about as unreachable as someone could be."

Matthew's mouth was agape. "Jeff's the only one with the codes? What sense does that make? He's never here! He goes on these tech-free retreats all the time. Why can't we just press the goddamn button ourselves?"

Stewart shook his head. "It's impossible. You can't issue a kill signal without the codes, and Jeff insisted that he be the final arbiter on a kill decision. No codes, no shutdown."

Matthew's fury returned, the vein in his forehead throbbing again. "This would *never* happen in a public company! It's just flat-out irresponsible not to have contingency plans for an emergency. I'm fucking stunned that I'm just learning about this now."

"We'll be lucky if five people want to ride in a Beemo after today," Sophie blurted out, giving voice to everyone's unspoken fear. "We're sitting here powerless while our car is killing pedestrians in Boston. Every minute it's on the road is another potential lawsuit. Our legal costs could make operational costs look like a rounding error."

Matthew rose and began pacing back and forth. When he spoke, there was determination in his slate-grey eyes. "We need to contact Jeff and get those shutdown codes. Srini may be our best hope for now, but we have to attack this across multiple fronts." He waved Melissa over. "Mel, it's probably pointless, but try calling Jeff. If it goes to voicemail, call Anna at the ranch and tell her she needs to drive up to the retreat with a satellite phone and laptop and interrupt him. Tell her it's an emergency."

The COO balled his hands into fists and placed them on the table. Looming over Stewart and Sophie, they could see his anger cooling to a steely resolve. "The wheels are in motion but there's no way of knowing how long it will take. We can wait for someone to save us or we can save ourselves. I vote for action, and I'm open to all ideas, even the crazy ones."

Stewart spoke up. "There *is* another option to consider," he said deliberately. "But nobody's going to like it."

XII.

Despite the music blasting at top volume, the sound of screaming pierced the Beemo's dark bubble before Will even felt the flat *thud* of flesh on metal. The taxi was cleaving its way through the sidewalk as terrified people scattered before it like ants.

He watched as the car pursued a young woman wearing a *Juicy* sweatshirt, quickly overtaking her and upending her body into the windshield where her head split like a ripe pineapple. Blood and matter clotted the front window, activating the Beemo's wipers and smearing gore across the glass in a grotesque finger painting.

Bodies were being tossed aside with a sickening crunch or falling beneath the tires and being run over. For some crazy reason, each bump reminded Will of the jutted country roads that he, Zac, and Alison drove to ski at Sugarbush. The horrible realization was that these weren't potholes but human beings. Brothers . . . sisters . . . husbands . . . people who would be missed and mourned. *Victims.*

The Beemo crashed through an empty (*thank God*) restaurant patio, sending plastic chairs and tables flying into the air. Ahead of them, people ran for their lives, some beelining straight into traffic in their desperation to escape the rampaging egg. Those too slow to react were simply run down and left motionless on the sidewalk, black tiremarks burned into their back like cattle brands.

Why the fuck isn't Beemo stopping the car?! Will's conversation with the tech had given him a glimmer of hope, but she'd obviously failed and now things were growing worse by the second. He *had* to do something. "Die you piece of shit," he whispered, tears welling up in his eyes. "Die Die DIE DIE DIE!" Anguish quickly gave way to a molten fury that burned through his body. Seeing red, Will snatched his briefcase from the floor and heaved it with all his might into the display. The impact caused the glass to splinter and he felt a small jolt of triumph: *I can hurt you too, fucker.*

Sensing his assault, the car suddenly accelerated with enough speed to toss him forcefully into the back seats. Turning to survey the damage behind him, Will was staggered by the sight.

This must be what a war zone looks like. Or a bomb explosion.

The sidewalk was an open wound, ripped apart in less than a minute of pure violence. Debris. Broken bodies. The cries of the wounded as they struggled to pull themselves to safety lest the car return. Sickened, Will turned away and caught sight of an older, well-dressed woman standing perfectly still, obviously frozen with fear as she watched the black egg hurtling toward her. *Move!* Will implored her silently, as the gap rapidly closed. She finally did, stepping back at the last moment but not quickly enough to avoid the side mirror, which caught her torso and spun her aside, probably breaking several ribs. *At least she's alive,* Will thought, watching the woman vomit blood as she writhed in pain on the ground. *That fur coat's going to need dry-cleaning.* The next victim, a man pedaling furiously on his bike, wasn't so lucky; killing him was child's play as the Beemo caught up with him easily and crushed both man and machine beneath its tires, compressing them into an indistinguishable heap of flesh and metal.

As the body count continued to pile up, Will didn't know how much more he could take. He'd read about PTSD and the effect it had on people who lived through traumatic events. Even if he survived, he'd probably be in therapy the rest of his life. He couldn't shake the feeling that there was a final space reserved just for him on the growing list of victims. He'd seen too much to get away scot-free. In every book and movie, the killer never leaves witnesses behind.

The sidewalk ended at a busy cross-street choked with morning traffic. The sight gave Will a small pang of optimism: *No way we're getting through that. There's nowhere for us to go. It has to stop.* His elation was tempered by the stark realization that the Beemo, faced with the impassable barrier, could simply turn around and make another brutal run along the sidewalk, finishing off any survivors. Instead, the car swung onto the road, jumped the median and launched itself into a row of oncoming traffic. Faced with a black missile speeding straight toward them, the approaching cars swerved and collided, adding to the enveloping chaos and confusion.

Amazingly, Will could see people pointing and running toward them, camera-phones held aloft, their instincts for self-preservation apparently overcome by a desire to capture the show. *Fucking idiots,* he thought, *you're putting yourselves in danger for a viral video. Get the hell away from here!* Will had seen enough to know that the car could decide in an instant to veer off course and begin mowing people down, and while there might have been some measure of Darwinian justice in it, he'd never root for more death.

As the Beemo veered in and out of traffic, the question of whether the car had a master plan or was simply running amok had occurred to Will. He struggled to grasp why its pre-programmed instincts had been superseded by a seemingly random projection of violence toward anything in its path. He guessed the earlier breakdown and strange antivirus messages had something to do with it. That seemed to be an inflection point after which things began spiraling out of control. Maybe its electronic brain was broken or a sick hacker had seized control of the car to cause as much murder and mayhem as possible? *Maybe maybe maybe.*

Unbeknownst to Will, the eighty-five ultrasonic sensors spaced along the Beemo's body were collecting every incoming signal and feeding these stimuli into a central CPU where navigation decisions were being made in a nanosecond, keeping the car two steps ahead of any human driver. When it detected small gaps in traffic, the car squeezed its way through. When no gaps existed, it simply created space by plowing into the other vehicles and knocking them aside like toys. The Beemo's boron steel frame was tempered with titanium and designed to take more punishment than commercial vehicles, and even larger SUVs were outmatched by its reckless brawn.

A construction obstacle course suddenly appeared in their path, forcing the Beemo to abandon the breakdown lane and instead steer into the median. Thrust to the inside, they became entangled in traffic. Frustrated, the car pulsed and whirred, pushing against the constraints like an enraged bull in a pen. While he wouldn't have dreamed of a high-speed escape attempt, their current predicament presented an opportunity that Will was determined to take. Standing straight up, he hammered at the STOP button, hoping against hope that it might suddenly activate and spring the door open, leaving him free to flee to safety. When it failed to respond (*of course*), he lashed out with a kick, and then another. *Open, goddamn you!* The door felt as unyielding as stone, not moving an inch under his furious barrage.

One horrified motorist, suddenly finding himself pressed against an aggressive and bloodstained Beemo, panicked and veered his car off the road, creating an opening in the flow of traffic. Will felt instant torque as the Beemo thrust itself through the gap, the sudden momentum so powerful that it carried them straight off the road. Continuing its forward motion, the car sped toward the grove of trees that separated the tranquility of Boston Common from the rest of the world. Will knew what lay beyond those trees: fifty acres of walking paths full of tourists and locals and students going about their days, exercising, reading, sitting on benches, walking their dogs, the morning sun warm upon their faces. The park offered little natural protection and would be a perfect killing field, he realized with horror. *Like sheep being herded down the chute for slaughter.*

Bowing his head, Will offered a quick prayer for the people ignorant to the terror now heading their way. He felt like he was slipping into numbness and despair . . . where any shred of hope was immediately obliterated. Then, in his moment of darkness, a sound came, so faint at first that it seemed imagined. As it grew louder and more definitive, it felt like a divine hand had reached out to him and pulled him back from the brink.

Sirens.

XIII.

"**M**el, hold on for a minute," Matthew said to Melissa, who was all too happy to refrain from speed-dialing Jeff and Anna to deliver bad news. Whatever Stewart's proposal was, the fact that he assumed a negative reception caused his colleagues to regard him with a mix of curiosity and suspicion.

While nobody would deny his brilliance, the CSO had never really fit into the executive suite. *Let the mad scientist tinker in his lab,* they whispered with self-satisfied smirks behind his back, *and leave the real work to the professionals.* Only now, the mad scientist's creation could bring them all down, and they needed every bit of knowledge in his head to avoid total catastrophe.

"Let's hear it," Matthew said, taking his seat.

Stewart spoke carefully. "We all agree that the car needs to be stopped. Srini's working on that now. But you're right, Matthew. There *are* no guarantees and time is working against us. It could take hours to reach Jeff and get the kill codes. The way I see it there's one more angle we could play. It's risky but it might solve our problem." He paused. "The police. We push the local authorities to take out the Zero."

Sophie expelled a sharp breath and Matthew's brow furrowed. Stewart could almost see their wheels turning. "How exactly would that work?" Matthew asked.

"We tell them the car's malfunctioning and out of control and we can't stop it. They'll be forced to throw everything they have at it until they succeed. We share its weak points and vulnerabilities and do whatever we can to help them kill *one* car so that we don't have to kill *fifteen thousand*."

There was a time when such a suggestion would have been unthinkable, but as their situation grew more desperate, Stewart could see his colleagues seriously considering his proposal. Matthew looked to Sophie and she made no overt moves to object.

"So we're admitting to law enforcement that we can't control our own vehicles? Isn't that negligence or an admission of guilt? What about liability, Sophie?"

Beemo's general counsel looked thoughtful. "Consider this . . . car companies issue recalls all the time. They admit fault, settle the lawsuits and move on. Remember Ford and the Pinto Memo? That was about as bad as it gets, but even that eventually blew over. Every major automaker has been through bigger crises with higher fatalities and they survived. We'd have to initiate an immediate recall, but . . . with message discipline and a slush fund for payoffs, I think we could survive."

The attitude shift in the room was palpable, yet Matthew remained skeptical. "I don't like the fact that we're giving up control," he objected. "It's risky. There's too much unpredictability. What if the police blow it?"

Stewart was blunt. "We don't *have* any control," he stated flatly. "We're not terminating our own efforts to stop the car, but let's face it—the cops are on the ground in Boston and we're not. They're in the best position to do the heavy lifting. We push them to take out the Zero and end all this."

He could see Matthew wavering. "I still don't like it," he said. Then he paused. "But I don't see any other viable alternatives." He motioned to Mel, who seemed to be constantly talking into her cell phone, and she hurried over. "Mel, change of plan. Get in touch with the Boston Police. Ask for a captain or someone in charge and tell them it's an emergency."

A momentary look of confusion passed across Mel's face. She held out her cell phone to Matthew. "I've already got them on the line. They called *us*."

XIV.

Even with an intimate knowledge of the timeless mystery that was Boston's traffic grid, Michael Finneran had come to rely on GPS to guide him. In a job where minutes could mean the difference between life and death, he couldn't afford to get stuck in traffic.

Now he found himself ducking in and out of side streets as GPS directed him around the gridlock, surely worsened by the growing number of crime scenes the Beemo was leaving in its wake. New calls were coming in every minute, and with a highly mobile suspect, Michael could only follow the trail and hope to put himself in the best position possible to intercept the car and stop its rampage.

Like most good cops, he had a finely sharpened sense of intuition; he referred to it affectionately as his "Spidey sense." Trusting his Spidey sense had saved Michael's life more than once, and right now it was telling him that the car would continue north toward the water. What troubled him was the fact that his adversary didn't think like a human. Because it couldn't, could it? It was a machine, and its unpredictability made it even more dangerous.

"Lieutenant, come in." *Sergeant Sullivan.*

Michael grabbed the receiver immediately. "I'm here. Go ahead, Sergeant."

"We just got a call from a civilian. Said he was sitting in traffic at Boylston and Charles when a Beemo came up from behind and sideswiped his car. Hit a couple of other cars too before taking off. The Beemo was a mess, he said, all banged up. It has to be our suspect."

Boylston and Charles, that's seven blocks away. "When did the call come in?"

"About three minutes ago."

That means it's still in the area. Glancing over his shoulder lest he cause his own crash, Michael swung an illegal U-turn to head in the opposite direction. "I'm close and can be there in five or six minutes. Alert our units in the area and let's see if someone can pick up pursuit."

"Yes, sir. There's one more thing, Lieutenant."

"What is it?" Michael asked, distracted by a slow-moving Amazon truck in his way. He chirped his siren and the truck pulled aside to let him pass.

"I have someone from Beemo HQ in Cupertino on the line. He says he's an executive and that he can help. Do you want me to patch him through?"

That got his attention. "Yes. Who is it?"

"His name is Matthew Palmer and he's the COO."

"Good job. Send him to my cell." Dropping the radio, Michael fished for the phone in his pocket as it rang. "This is Lieutenant Michael Finneran with the Boston Police Department. With whom am I speaking?"

"Lieutenant?" the man on the other end asked, sounding distant. "This is Matthew Palmer with the Beemo Corporation. Can you hear me?"

"Yes, Mr. Palmer. I can hear you."

"Lieutenant, you also have Sophie Chin and Stewart Wheeler listening in on speakerphone. We're part of the executive team here at Beemo and we want to help you get this situation under control as quickly as possible."

Michael had no time for polite civilian protocol. "You can start by telling me *exactly how to stop your goddamn car*."

XV.

When he first heard the approaching sirens, Will felt as if a dark curtain had been drawn aside ever so slightly, allowing in a small beam of light: hope. *The cops are coming. They'll help me.*

He prayed they'd find him soon, because right now the Beemo was on a direct crash course with the busiest public garden in Boston. It had plunged headlong into the wooded grove and was steering through a slalom course of elms and willows, the low-hanging branches swatting at the windows as dead wood cracked beneath the tires. Tree cover grew thinner and thinner until they reached the edge of the Common and burst into the open space. Skidding to a stop on the dewy morning grass, the Beemo seemed to be surveilling the area. This corner of the park was remote, tranquil even, and Will could see only a few people milling about, none paying any attention to the bruised and muscular taxi that suddenly appeared in their midst. Will strained to listen for the sirens and was distressed to find their sound fading. *We lost them. They're looking for us on the street, not here.*

His attention turned to a blond woman walking briskly along the footpath, totally engaged with the phone in her hands, oblivious to everything else. Silent as a black panther, the Beemo rolled forward, falling in line behind her. The acid began to rise in Will's throat. Although the car's aggression was contained, he knew what was coming next.

Oh God please no, not her too.

Slipping out of his shoulder harness, Will stood and began pounding on the windows, screaming to get the woman's attention. "HEY, YOU, LOOK UP! HEY! YOU'RE IN DANGER! LISTEN TO ME!" His throat strained with the effort of yelling, but the car's airtight compartment easily swallowed up his words, rendering them ineffective. *Fuck your goddamn phone, look up already!* Bracing himself, Will lashed out with a kick to the shattered display, then another one. The car ignored him and focused on the prey ahead. Hopelessly still lost in her digital world, the woman remained completely unaware of the predator stalking her. They'd drawn close enough to her so Will could recognize the distinctive pattern of the Coach bag on her arm. He continued to call out and flail at the windows as the speedometer ticked higher and higher. *No No No NO NO!*

The woman heard nothing and saw nothing until the car was on top of her. It surged forward to knock her to the ground, grinding her body beneath the chassis and dragging her twenty feet before spitting her out. The cold-blooded assassination seemed to nourish the car; it vibrated with power and energy, bounding forward to leave the bloody trail and mangled corpse in its wake. Inside, the frantic notes of "Flight of the Bumblebee" poured forth over the speakers while externally, the car's horn began to blare incessantly, loudly proclaiming the car's presence and scaring the shit out of anyone unlucky enough to be in its path. Parkgoers jumped up from their benches and hid behind trees, pointing and shouting as the black egg sped past them. *At least it's not running people over*, Will thought, but the thought didn't quite sit right. *What's it up to?* Something wasn't connecting. Why sneak up soundlessly behind the blond woman and then become a noisy spectacle that people could hear a mile away? It didn't make sense, and the lack of reason was driving Will insane.

Nearby, crowds formed as morning walkers and curious onlookers rushed up to share the unusual sight of a robotic taxi speeding along the footpath. Watching the people congregate, Will had a sudden revelation: *It's drawing them out. There weren't enough people, so it's purposely drawing a crowd. When there's enough, it'll turn and cut them down like a scythe.*

Waves of nausea washed over him. *Not more killing. Please.* He felt feeble, ineffective—a pawn in a bizarre game without rules. Forced to bear witness to its atrocities, Will was convinced the Beemo wouldn't cease killing until an overpowering force stopped it, crushing it into a block of metal or dousing it in gasoline and setting it alight. Anything less and the body count would keep piling up and there wasn't a thing Will or the cops or the Beemo people could do about it because everyone had failed.

Then there was the question of his *own* safety. The car would surely meet a violent end, so how exactly could Will prevent *himself* from becoming collateral damage? He had every intention of going home to his wife and son. Although he'd damaged the monitor, the car was obviously built to take abuse and his attacks were increasingly futile. *Think, Will, think . . . what can you do?*

Still loudly cranking classical music and sounding its horn, the Beemo's speedometer crept up past fifty, and Will realized that he should sit back down and buckle himself in. People, trees and benches flew by in a blur. Terrified parkgoers simply dropped their possessions and ran. The car clipped a metal lamppost, passing through it like wet tissue and sending it crashing to the ground. They smashed into an abandoned child's stroller and collided with a hotdog cart, knocking it over and sending its green umbrella spinning across the lawn. The Zero plowed through a row of tables stacked with t-shirts (*Celtics Pride, I♥ Boston!*) that fluttered down to the ground like falling leaves.

Having crisscrossed the park's entire length, they were fast approaching the northern corner where stone steps led to the golden dome of the State House.

As it approached the stone wall, the car veered sharply onto the grass and skidded into a perfect 180-degree turn, its grill pointing back toward the trail of wreckage. Poised to make another charge, the power gauge flared from green to red and the entire frame shook with barely-contained energy. Will noticed people peering out from behind trees and benches, watching the Beemo warily and probably contemplating if they should make a break for it. He didn't like their chances. *Don't do it,* he thought. *It will kill you.* He couldn't believe there weren't more fatalities on the car's pass through the park. The human toll of a second high-speed tear through the park would be catastrophic, Will thought, and witnessing more death and carnage might just break him.

The Beemo had shown its unpredictability time and time again and it did so anew, not storming forward as Will had expected, but advancing slowly, its electric motor a whisper. Like a languid cobra, its tongue darting out to taste the air, the car wound along the footpath, sensors picking up every heat signal and scintilla of movement and conveying these back to the CPU, where they were processed and pulsed back to the drive system. This visualization suddenly crystalized the Beemo's intentions and confirmed Will's worst fears.

It's hunting.

XVI.

When Melissa first offered Matthew her phone, he snapped his fingers and pointed to the table. "Put the call through to speaker." The conference room, fully wired for video and sound, was at once filled with the angry voice of an agitated Boston Police lieutenant at top volume:

"You can start by telling me exactly how to stop your goddamn car."

It was like tossing a grenade into the room. The executives sat mute, glancing at each other nervously. They were used to a certain amount of deference, and no one had ever heard a police officer speak that way. Without letting them respond, Finneran continued. "I'm the Officer-in-Charge for District D4 in Boston and I'm in pursuit of one of your taxis, which is responsible for at least one fatality and multiple other injuries. I just left the accident scene and saw the victim myself, a kid no more than twenty-two. I've got every cop in the city out searching for your car and I want to know why you haven't shut the damn thing down already."

Matthew leaned toward the microphone. "We're doing everything we can, Lieutenant. There's a malfunction that's temporarily caused the car to stop responding to our directives."

The air crackled. "You mean you *can't* shut it down?"

Matthew cleared his throat before speaking. "At the moment, yes. That's right. Yes."

"Pardon my French, Mr. Palmer, but that's fucked up. You have what—hundreds?—of robot taxis driving in my city and you can't respond when they blow a fuse? There's a passenger in the car, too, you know. His name's Will Butler. All I care about is getting Will out of there safely and stopping the car before more people get hurt or killed. Now how in the name of all that's holy are we going to prevent your car from hurting more people?"

Matthew looked around helplessly. Everyone knew this call would be difficult, but the acidic tone of the lieutenant's words still stunned them. This qualified as a genuine, no-holds-barred fiasco; nobody expected to escape the madness unscathed.

Sensing an opening, Stewart gestured to Matthew. He nodded, and Stewart leaned forward. "Lieutenant Finneran, this is Dr. Wheeler. I design and oversee all of our AVs. Perhaps I could provide something that would help."

"Go ahead."

Sophie flipped the phone console button to MUTE. "Be careful," she hissed.

I'm three steps ahead of you, Sophie. Stewart clicked the button back to TALK. "We do know about the passenger and believe me his safety and the safety of the public is our top priority. We have a number of safeguards built into the vehicle to stop it in the event of an emergency, but there's an unexpected malfunction preventing us from asserting control over the car. We're working like hell to fix it, but right now we don't have an answer. Our fallback position is to broadcast what's called a kill signal, but we need our CEO's approval to do this and he's . . . on sabbatical and currently unreachable. We're working through every contingency in our playbook to bring this situation under control, but I can't guarantee results or give you a timetable. As much as I hate to admit it, that's the reality of our position."

The line went quiet as Michael contemplated Stewart's statement. Faintly, a police siren wailed in the background. Although he hadn't revealed it, Stewart knew some things about Lieutenant Finneran. The Lieutenant had been the point person on a homicide case last year that was splashy enough to make national news, and Stewart had followed the case. His take on Finneran was that of a classic alpha male who would not be content to sit on the sidelines and hope for the best. No, Michael Finneran would seize the mantle of control. Stewart was betting that his carefully-worded *mea culpa* would lead Finneran to an inevitable conclusion: that it would be up to him to stop their car.

When the lieutenant spoke again, it was with an air of impatient authority. "Unfortunately, Dr. Wheeler, we can't wait for you to get it right. If you're not in a position to act, then BPD needs to step in and handle the situation. Let's start by you telling me everything I need to know about your car."

Stewart exchanged a knowing look with his colleagues. *The gun's loaded. Now, we need to point it.* "As I see it, the best options are containment or destruction. Containment means cutting off the car's ability to move. Trap it in an alley or surround it and then block the escape routes. If you can arrest its movements you can disable the car and rescue the passenger. But it won't be easy: the car is designed to protect itself. I can't say exactly how it might respond to . . . provocations, given its current malfunction."

"What about destruction?"

"There are vulnerabilities you can exploit."

"Such as?"

"Target the wheels. A direct hit on the wheel well from another vehicle could smash the tire and damage the electric drive unit. The chassis is steel-reinforced and as tough as they come, but the Beemo's fundamentally like any other car. It needs its wheels to move. Take the wheels out and it becomes a three-ton paperweight."

"The wheels," Michael repeated aloud, his mind already working. "We can't shoot at the tires because that puts the passenger at risk. But we could use spike strips."

"Negative. Spike strips won't work. Our tires can't be punctured because they're not rubber. We use airless tires made of polyurethane and glass-reinforced plastic. Really strong stuff. We didn't want our fleet held up by trivial matters like flat tires, so we made them indestructible to most road debris. But they *won't* stand up the application of blunt force. Like a direct hit from another vehicle."

"Before we take it out, we need to find your car first, Dr. Wheeler. You must have the capacity to track it . . . can you tell me its location right now?"

"Unfortunately, no. The tracking chip's not signaling—probably collateral damage from the system malfunction." Stewart didn't mention his suspicions that the car *itself* was probably blocking the signal to prevent them from tracking its movements. *BPD doesn't need to know all the inside details, do they?*

"Is there any way to know where it might be going?"

"The last known destination was Logan Airport before things went . . . sideways. As far as where it's going or how it's making navigation decisions, we're in the dark. I can tell you our cars use commercial GPS to navigate, so it's seeing the same traffic patterns that you and I would see. It's also hard-coded to avoid traffic and congestion, so it will always prioritize travel on open roads. You should know that."

"Noted. How worried should I be about the car running over more people?"

The question sent an uneasy ripple through the conference room. "I don't know," Stewart confessed. "This has never happened before."

"Is it just the one car?" Michael asked. "What about all the other Beemos?"

I have to give him credit, Stewart thought. *He's as sharp as I thought.* "As far as we can tell, the malfunction is isolated to a single vehicle."

"What else should I know?"

"Its top speed is 200 mph, so don't try to outrun it. You can't. You're better off setting up roadblocks and surrounding and assaulting it when it's forced to slow down."

Michael had a lot more questions for Stewart, but he needed time to think and plan and direct his officers. "I have to hang up now, but here's my cell number. Call me if you can think of anything else that might be useful. Anything at all." He rattled off a series of digits, which Stewart committed to memory and Matthew wrote down on the back of his hand.

Matthew jumped back into the conversation, obviously relieved that the call was wrapping up. "Of course we will, Lieutenant, and we appreciate your understanding. It's a regrettable situation for all of us, and we're as shocked and heartbroken as you by what's happened today."

Michael's voice went cold. "It's not over yet, Mr. Palmer. I appreciate the information, but don't think for a second that I don't hold all of you responsible for that boy's death. My people are out here risking their lives because folks like you built a machine that *you* can't control and now it's on a crime spree in my city. Believe me when I tell you there *will* be an investigation once this is over and I *will* make sure justice gets served." He paused. "Thank you for your time."

The line went dead and the conference room was silent. None of the Beemo executives moved a muscle, each consumed by their own thoughts. In Stewart's mind, there were no good outcomes at this point—just some that could be less bad than others. Even the car's destruction at the hands of the BPD couldn't fix what had already been broken. These ruminations began leading Stewart to a foreign place . . . one in which morality was more transactional and the lines blurred between wrong and right. Because as much as he tried, Dr. Stewart Wheeler just couldn't bring himself to care more about the car's victims than his own rapidly-declining fortunes.

XVII.

The Beemo advanced in stealth mode, deliberately creeping along the paved footpath and shifting direction as its sensors picked up new signals. Will was relieved to see that the park had nearly emptied, and guessed that a firsthand observation of the Beemo's destruction was enough to send most people fleeing.

Then something new caused his apprehension to spike: the Beemo had steered off the footpath and was now advancing over the grass toward a previously-untouched part of the Common, far away from the recent pandemonium. There, nobody would know what the Beemo had done or what it could do. *They'll have no idea what's coming their way.*

The car crested a small hill where a vast expanse of green grass spilled out before them. As it descended with purpose, more and more people came into view. A group of joggers moved toward them on the footpath, conversing back and forth and blissfully enjoying the day. The car sensed the pack immediately, shifting course to intercept them. In a few seconds the runners came face-to-face with the bloodstained and battered Beemo. At first there was confusion, then full-blown panic as the group broke apart and scattered in all directions.

A man in green sweatpants with a white stripe scrambled up the branches of a young elm, which immediately sagged under his weight. Accelerating, the car targeted him and slammed head-on into the tree, sending him airborne. Stunned but intact, he tumbled to the ground as the Beemo gunned the transmission in reverse to disengage its bumper. Pulling away, it spun forward to pursue the fleeing figure. The man was so distracted watching the speeding Beemo behind him that he ran smack into a lamppost—like a character in a cruel cartoon—knocking himself to the ground. Dazed, he lifted his head just in time to see the car's mangled grill descending upon him, snuffing him out with lethal efficiency. In a gruesome flourish, the Beemo backed up to run over the dead man again, then peeled forward toward the heart of the Common where horrified parkgoers were just beginning to grasp what was happening.

The brutality of the man's death was unbearable. Will was livid. He couldn't bring himself to gaze upon another lifeless body on the ground. Unclipping his seat belt to stand up straight, he braced himself and continued his assault on the broken route display, doing his best to ram his foot through the splintered glass. "YOU MURDEROUS SHIT I'LL SMASH YOU TO PIECES!" Before he could aim another kick, the Beemo swerved and sent him tumbling to the floor. He scrambled back up to see the car pursue three more joggers who had splintered from the pack, now sprinting like their lives depended on it toward an elevated concrete bandstand. *I've been up on that stage before,* Will thought. *Alison and I climbed it while Zac rode his bike. Back when things were normal.* Will buckled himself in as the car increased its speed, obviously intent on running over the trio before they reached safety.

On a day already filled with tragic loss, they were among the lucky ones. With the Beemo hot on their heels, the runners ascended the bandstand steps and quickly disappeared behind its stone pillars. The Beemo's momentum carried it squarely into the bandstand's foundation, where it collided brutally, hurtling Will forward in his seat belt and forcing the air violently from his lungs. Its front end crumpled, the Beemo bounced back, dented but far from finished. Slamming into reverse, it darted backward to create distance and then jerked to a stop, fully prepared to make another charge.

Then, like a scene from a movie, the cavalry arrived: a black-and-white police car appeared out of nowhere and skidded to a stop between the Beemo and the bandstand. Surprised by the sudden intrusion, the car hesitated, its power gauge cooling from angry red to green as it simmered in place.

The sirens—they finally found us! Thank God, the police are here! Will knew that where there was one cop, there would soon be more, yet this small reassurance was tempered by a realization: the police presence *could* trigger an escalation in hostilities that would put him in even more danger.

The Beemo shifted left and began circling the bandstand like a shark sighting its prey. The police car moved with it, mirroring the Beemo's movements but showing no aggression and keeping a safe distance. *It's testing them,* Will thought. *Testing their reaction and looking for an opening.* The strange dance continued for another full rotation before the Beemo rolled to a stop. Will's eyes scanned the horizon, searching desperately for a rescue party but there was none. *Where the fuck is everybody?*

From the inside, a low hum sounded over the car's speaker and then the disembodied robotic voice Will had grown to hate slurred drunkenly:

"WE'VE ARRIVED AT OUR DESTINATION WILL BUT-LERRRRRRR . . . "

And then in a second everything shut down. Again. Engine, electronics, lights—all dead. The police car waited, its flashing lights the only sign of movement. *What the fuck's the car up to now? Did the last collision finally do it in?* Fearful that this was a trick, Will sat motionless in the stale air for a full five minutes before slowly reaching down to click open his seat belt. Cautiously he pressed the door release. Nothing. The Beemo may have been dormant, but it wasn't about to let its prisoner escape that easily.

Still a captive, Will out stared at the empty Common and wondered when the rest of the troops would arrive. Unless he could produce a miracle, the BPD was now his best chance of survival. His fear, however, was that they would underestimate their opponent. He had knowledge to share but no means of communicating with would-be rescuers. *They still don't know how ruthless and sadistic the car really is. The body count will keep growing, I'm sure of it. How does anyone stop something so mindless, so nihilistic? How do I get home to my family alive?* The pieces weren't adding up, and as hard as he tried, Will just couldn't fathom the end game.

XVIII.

They're hiding something, Michael Finneran decided.

After he ended his call with the Beemo executives, Michael felt his blood boil. He was a seasoned interrogator who could sniff out deception like a bloodhound, even over the phone. They weren't telling him everything. It was implausible to believe they couldn't stop their own car, so why lie? How does a simple malfunction turn an AV into a killer? Their willingness to evade responsibility was disheartening; the Beemo people were almost *eager* to clear this nasty business off their plate and let him clean up the mess. It angered him to think that his fellow officers and the people of Boston—*his* people—would be paying the price for their mistake. "Protect and Serve" weren't just words; they were ideals that guided Michael's actions every day. His strong moral compass was one of the reasons that he had been drawn to police work, and the glaring deficiencies exhibited by the Beemo executives only confirmed to him that corporate America was a cesspool of depravity that valued absolutely nothing beyond the almighty dollar.

Michael could hear the radio chatter beginning to pick up:

"... reports of a pedestrian struck on Tremont Street ... "

"... ambulance requested, corner of Beacon and Kent ... vehicle hit and run ... "

" . . . A one-four-three by the Emerson Colonial Theatre, multiple casualties reported . . . unit five-five, can you respond . . . ?"

He was stunned by the sheer magnitude of violence the car was perpetrating across the city. With each report his apprehension grew. What would happen when they finally confronted the car? He'd been serving the public for more than twenty years and was used to dealing with the darker side of humanity. The blue wall would always be stronger than the malevolent forces pushing against it—he truly believed that—but this situation was unique. Michael feared his team wasn't equipped to handle this kind of threat. They'd succeed eventually, through the sheer application of force, if nothing else, but it terrified him to think about how much pain had to be endured first. At least you could despise bad people, but a machine . . . it was just a thing. Perfectly sociopathic. Soulless. Terrifying.

Containment or destruction.

Contain or destroy. Two choices. Neither of them great.

In his mind, containment was preferable since it presented less risk to his people. The downside was that it required planning and numbers, and the Beemo's string of crime scenes across the city would make assembling an overwhelming force even more difficult. His officers would be responding to a flood of incoming calls about hit-and-run victims with life-threatening or even fatal injuries. Casualties had to be dealt with first; you couldn't leave bodies lying in the street.

That meant destruction. For now, firearms were out of the question; too risky to the Beemo's passenger. But was there a point where collateral damage was acceptable to save lives? He could call in heavy ordinance to blow up the car, but that meant taking Will Butler with it, and Michael wasn't that desperate yet. They could try weaponizing their vehicles. For once, Michael was thankful that SUVs made up the bulk of the department's motor pool. A single SUV could, theoretically, damage the Beemo as a gang of SUVs smashed it into submission. There were risks, of course. Could he really order his officers to deliberately crash their vehicles into another car? These were murky waters with moral and legal implications (and questions), but that didn't mean he wouldn't do it himself. Then he thought of Suzie. The local news must have caught wind of this story by now, and he wondered how long it would be until Suzie texted him about it. *If she knew what I was planning, she'd take me out herself.* Michael pushed the thought aside. *Don't get distracted, Mikey. Focus on the job at hand. Emotions lead to mistakes.*

The radio crackled and the words Michael had been waiting to hear all morning finally rose above the static: "*Urgent, this is Unit five-four, requesting backup at the intersection of Beacon and Park. We have a visual on the suspect, a heavily damaged Beemo taxicab. Suspect has entered the Common and is now parked on the footpath. No sign of movement at this time . . . we're in position to pursue it if it runs.*"

Michael seized the radio. "Five-four, this is Lieutenant Finneran. I'm en route and I want you to stay put for now and do not engage. Repeat, keep the vehicle in your sight but do not engage. All available units requested to respond to Beacon and Park. Surround and contain the suspect until backup arrives. Deadly force is not, repeat *not* approved at this time."

Less than ten minutes away, Michael thought. He swung up a side street to avoid traffic and pressed down hard on the accelerator, streamlining through the narrow alley. A cascade of scenarios played out in his head, almost all of which involved smashing his Vic into the fugitive Beemo to disable it. He would hate to wreck the Vic, but he'd do it in a second to save lives . . . his own safety be damned. He'd been to the hospital before. No big deal. Most times.

Still, the doubts persisted. *We're not ready for this.* Their response had to be perfect; the cost of failure meant more dead citizens and maybe some cops hurt, too. Declan's voice sounded in his head: *Always have a backup plan, Mikey. The best-laid plans go to shit the second you kick the door in. You've gotta give yourself options, even if they're all bad ones.*

He knew Boston Common intimately and called up a mental picture. A few major roads in and out. Lots of people, mostly pedestrians. Wide open space without many barriers to stop a speeding car. *What if it runs?* It would be disastrous to have the car drive through the park; better to keep it on narrow surface streets. Geographically, the area looked like a clenched fist punching into the water, so pushing the car north would lead to natural choke points as roads merged into bridges. That could be advantageous; a bridge was easier to secure and contain than a roadway. Fewer escape routes and less pedestrians to worry about.

Then it hit him: *the evacuation routes.* In the event of a terrorist attack or natural disaster, Boston's city planners had drawn up emergency evacuation routes. The goal was to create a free-flowing pipeline that would stream traffic out of the city, and Beacon Street was one of these major exit routes. *Plus we already have the evac protocols, and I can use those.* Evacuation routes could address the *where,* but that still left the *how.* If the car fled, he couldn't control its direction, and there was no guarantee he could direct it down Beacon Street. *Think . . . think.* Playing back his conversation with the Beemo people, Michael suddenly had an idea.

He flipped the radio to a private channel and contacted Sergeant Sullivan. "Sergeant, call the Stateys. We're going to need their help because I want the main roads surrounding the Common closed down and blocked: Charles and Boylston. The second thing—and this is important—tell them *not* to clear the traffic first. Just shut it all down. I want traffic in that area jammed up for blocks and every pissed-off commuter pulling out their phone and complaining on their traffic app. The Beemo people said their car navigates with GPS, so we're going to manufacture a traffic crisis and push this car in the direction *we* choose. Copy that, Sergeant?"

"I'll get it done, Lieutenant."

Michael continued. "Last thing, the one road we leave *clear* is Beacon Street westbound from Boston Common to the Storrow Drive on-ramp. The suspect won't have any choice but to head north on Storrow. When it gets to the Zakim, we'll be waiting. I've got to make all the arrangements, so call me if you hit any snags. Over." Clicking off the radio, Michael picked up his phone and found the private cell number for Bob Mason. Bob was an old friend and he also happened to be the executive director of the MBTA, which meant that Bob controlled all public transit in Greater Boston. He dialed and after a few rings, Bob picked up.

"Mikey, it's been too long. You finally decide to ditch the cops and join the dedicated public servants?"

"Listen, Bob, I need a favor, and it's a big one . . . " Michael quickly explained his plan. The more he spoke, the crazier it sounded, yet Bob listened patiently. By the time he had finished, Michael was sure Bob was wishing he had chosen another groomsman for his wedding and let his old friend's call ring straight through to voicemail.

"Wow, that's a huge ask, Mike. I've never had to do anything like that, not on the kind of scale you're talking about. And the timeline . . . shit. Can you at least tell me what's happening?"

"You know I can't share the details, Bob—it's an active police operation. But I *can* tell you I wouldn't be asking unless it was a matter of life or death."

"Still, Mike, I mean . . . every active MBTA bus? I've got . . . *forty-two* of them running at every point in the city right now."

"Do you have the authority to do this yourself, Bob?"

"Well, sure, I do, but that's not the point . . . I can't . . . I can't just . . . "

"Lives are at stake and time's working against us, Bob. This is *me* talking. I can't do this without your help."

Michael held his breath as the line went silent. A small drop of sweat slid down the back of his neck. If Bob said no, all bets were off.

"I'll have to scramble, Mike. Let me make some calls and work out the contingency plans. I'll see what I can get done."

The feeling of relief was overwhelming. "Thanks buddy," Michael said. "I owe you one." Dropping the phone on his seat, he gripped the wheel and accelerated as he turned onto Beacon. *Almost there.* Through the tightly-packed rows of brick townhouses, he saw a flash of green—Boston Common. Michael approached a gap in the wrought-iron fence where vehicles could slip through and enter the park. Wary of pedestrians and not knowing what to expect, Michael made his way carefully along the footpath, taking note of the eerie silence, unusual for a weekday morning. *They're all scared of the car. Good. This is the last place I want people around today.*

It didn't take long before the suspect came into view. The Beemo sat in the middle of the Common, beat-up and motionless, like a junker that some drunk had abandoned on the grass the night before and forgotten about. A lone cruiser was parked facing it, and Michael was surprised that it was just the two of them. *Where are the good guys?* Guiding the Vic across the grass, he pulled alongside the other prowler and stopped. He thought briefly of killing his engine, but decided against it. He didn't want to be caught unprepared if the Beemo made a run for it.

Looks like we've got ourselves a standoff, Michael thought. *But where the hell is my backup?* Peering closely at the Beemo's scarred black windshield, he could imagine Will Butler sitting inside staring back at him. Unless Will was already dead, of course. The Beemo wasn't giving up any of its secrets. Michael needed more of everything: cars, cops, and time, but he doubted the Beemo would simply sit idly by and let him gain the upper hand. No, the car would fight back, and despite Michael's best efforts, there was a real possibility that the next chapter in this story would be penned in blood and haunt him for the rest of his life.

XIX.

In the cloistered stillness of the Beemo bubble, Will despaired for good news, and recent developments had given him newfound optimism. The cops were beginning to arrive and soon there would be more. Also, for the first time in a long time, his world was quiet.

That goddamn music! It was like the car was creating a soundtrack for its atrocities, alternating between blasting music at deafening levels and shuffling through its library of sound-effects, which included fighting cats and machine-gun fire. Played at maximum volume, the noise had ground like sandpaper on his already-frayed nerves. With everything now apparently in total shutdown, the silence was a blessing.

The carnage in the park left Will questioning if he could handle seeing another dead body. The drumming behind his temples beat with renewed ferocity and he thought he might be teetering on the edge of some sort of breakdown. He could still think rationally (at least he thought he could), but it felt like he'd been through a war. Horrific images of death played repeatedly, searing themselves into his psyche. If he lived through the day, he knew there would be permanent scars. Only yesterday his life had been so easy and normal. It saddened him that the Will Butler who had climbed into the Beemo that morning didn't exist anymore . . . one more casualty in a day filled with tragedy.

Faintly, from somewhere within the car, a muted whirring noise started up and then grew louder. A small light he hadn't noticed before began to blink red on the dashboard. With renewed horror, he realized that the car still maintained some flicker of life. *Something's happening . . . it's not dead yet.* As Will pondered this, he suddenly recalled skimming an interview with Beemo's CEO in an in-flight magazine. Among the executive's many brash statements was one that now leapt out at him: the promise that Beemo would soon be introducing a fleet of self-sufficient robotaxis with never-seen-before innovations, including a shadow repair system that would fix routine problems on its own, no humans required. As the whirring continued, Will realized with a jolt that the future was *already* here, and he was sitting in it. *It's fixing itself. The car's fixing itself.*

Given the amount of damage it had already absorbed, Will was hoping the Beemo would reach a point of no return and just die right there on the Common. Instead, the car clearly had other ideas. Still driven by whatever mission propelled its twisted electronic brain, it soldiered on. The game wasn't over yet—for all he knew it was still early innings—and Will feared that the car would soon become operable and burn out of there to continue its mission of mayhem.

The revelation quickly killed his budding optimism, leaving him defeated. The end wasn't in sight at all. He would likely die painfully as collateral damage in this suffocating compartment. And under "Cause of death" in his report, the coroner would write "robot taxi on a suicide mission." *That* was sure to be a first. Emotions washed over him . . . fear, anger, regret, sadness . . . not just for himself but also for the poor souls snuffed out and left in the street. He wished he'd been able to see Zac and Alison one last time. His vision clouded with tears as the enormity of the day's events rushed in to fill his head and heart.

He grieved for himself and the victims and their families, whose lives would never be the same.

He'd heard it said that in moments of great despair there can be light, and for Will the light was blue and flashing and perched atop a muscular grey car that had just pulled up to join the lone patrol car. It was a no-nonsense vehicle that someone important would drive, like Dirty Harry. Squinting at the vague silhouette of the man in the driver's seat, Will knew instinctively that this was *him*—the Man in Charge. The person who would either save Will's life or get him killed.

I've been waiting for you, Will thought. *Now you need to hurry because I know something you don't know: the car won't be here for long.*

Michael dared not drive his Crown Vic closer to the Beemo, fearful that any sudden or aggressive movement could break the tenuous calm. He needed to buy time. All over the city, courtesy of Bob Mason, resources were being mobilized to contain the Beemo and save lives, but nothing on that scale happened immediately.

His top priority was containment. Surround the Beemo and cut off its means of escape. With more officers and vehicles, they could move in to disable it and rescue the passenger, although he wasn't quite sure yet how this operation would work. The Beemo was still an enigma. While the tactics and reasoning were sound, his Spidey sense was tingling. *Expect the worst.*

Cautiously opening the Vic's door, Michael stepped outside to get a better look. The Beemo was a mess; its front end was heavily damaged and smeared with filth and a thick sludge that he guessed was coagulated blood ringed its windshield. There were no signs of movement from within. If Will Butler was still alive he'd have been through hell. *The car's really smashed up*, he thought. *A few well-placed hits from the Vic would crumple what's left of the front end and maybe take it out of action. The tires . . . target the tires. The car's not invulnerable and that means we've got a chance.*

Two black-and-whites approached slowly from the south. *Thank God.* Michael held up his hands to wave them into position and they fanned out across the perimeter. A state police prowler had also joined their ranks, giving the Stateys their first dog in the fight. Slowly and steadily their numbers grew, forming a wall of blue. Michael deliberately left a gap in the perimeter facing out toward Beacon Street, calculating that if the car were to run, it would follow the path of least resistance rather than trying to crash through the police cordon. What rattled him was the uncertainty that this suspect would follow any kind of rational playbook. He knew full well that any deviation from the route he'd planned could be disastrous, and the success of the operation could hinge on what happened here.

Michael spoke into the radio. "All units, this is Lieutenant Finneran. Maintain position and keep your distance from the suspect. We surround and contain for now until more cars arrive. The passenger's condition is still unknown, so report back if you see any signs of life inside the car." He paused as another cruiser approached, then waved it toward the left flank as reinforcement. Michael did a quick count. *Five so far . . . six with me. It's not enough. Not yet.* "When more officers arrive, we'll fill the gap and close in like a fist. No firearms; we can't risk it with the passenger. All units acknowledge."

"This is unit five-five, acknowledging . . ." One by one, each attending officer confirmed Michael's order. While this may have minimized the threat of errant bullets, Michael remained deeply concerned. *Six cars. I've been here almost twenty minutes and I only have six cars. I need twice that many.*

Hard experience had taught him that circumstances could change in a second if the Beemo decided to make a break for it. The backup plan was in motion, but so much depended on variables beyond his control. The car's lack of humanity worried him the most. Human beings, at least, were driven by universal instincts like logic and self-preservation that lent at least some predictability. A machine possessed none of these. *Nobody* really knew what was driving the Beemo or what its next move would be. He was loath to admit he had almost no control over the situation. The car was in control.

And why the fuck was it just sitting there? If the Beemo people had succeeded in killing it, why hadn't someone notified him? The BPD trained incessantly and developed guidelines for every type of scenario, but no playbook existed for killer robot cars. He was flying blind, relying on instinct and experience and adrenaline. *God help us if it runs before we're ready.*

Michael drummed his fingers on the hood and scanned the surrounding landscape. He could hear more sirens in the distance. The Beemo remained rooted in place, still dangerous, lying in wait like a wounded dinosaur that had crawled out of the primordial ooze. Michael was determined not to let it out of his sight, even for a second.

The cavalry will arrive . . . you can bet on that. A few more cars and it will be time to end you. That's a promise.

XXI.

Although Stewart's plan to have the BPD assume responsibility had gone as intended, the call had put everyone in a foul mood. Matthew didn't attempt to hide his agitation as he pushed the speakerphone toward Stewart.

"We need to talk to Srini," he commanded. Stewart dialed the number and the sound of ringing filled the conference room until Srini picked up.

"It's Stewart. I'm with Matthew and Sophie. What's the latest?"

Srini sounded stressed but rational. "Still nothing. The Zero's in full self-protection mode, but I'm running a program that probes for entry points faster than its security system can plug them up. I'll get in eventually, but we did too good a job making it impregnable. This is taking longer than I thought."

"Time is the last thing we have." Matthew's forehead vein was pulsing again.

"I *did* identify what I think is the root of the problem," Srini said. The executives sat up straight. He had their attention. "I downloaded the log files to trace all activity since this morning. What I found is that the antivirus program went crazy twenty minutes after picking up the passenger. It overrode the drive system and forced the car to pull over while it redirected all battery power toward ID'ing the virus. System scans are all negative until it checks the thermal imaging system, and that's when virus alerts pop up all over the place. But here's the thing: there never *was* a virus. I checked it myself. It's a ghost in the machine. There's definitely a big, big problem, but I'm positive it's not a virus."

"Then how do you explain what's happening?" Matthew asked.

"I'll show you. Look at this." Srini took control of the conference AV system and projected an image on the massive screen. "This is a thermogram I pulled from the Zero. What you're seeing is how the car sees the world. Trees, buildings, street signs . . . anything lacking a heat signal shows up as blue. Anything warm-blooded, like a human, generates a red image. The drive algorithm is hard-coded to avoid impact with red images no matter what, even if it has to run off a cliff. That's our insurance policy to make sure our cars never strike a human being."

Srini paused. "Only I didn't pull this picture from thermal imaging . . . I pulled it from the antivirus program. Whatever this glitch is, it's telling the car that every red image is a virus. Antivirus has taken control and assigned a new primary directive: eradicate the viruses at all costs."

Matthew and Sophie looked as though they were still processing the news, but Stewart knew immediately what this meant. Shocked, he stared at the haunting image on the screen, taken less than an hour ago, showing a crowded Boston street with red silhouettes everywhere. "So you're telling us *the Zero sees every person as a virus that needs to be eliminated?*"

For what seemed like a long time, Srini's shallow breathing over the speakers was all that could be heard. "Yes," he rasped.

The revelation was like a rancid tsunami crashing over the room. Everyone sat in stunned silence. For Stewart, it was like watching his worst nightmare come to life. *It's not an accident. The Zero's deliber-*

ately killing people. A machine like that could kill fifty, a hundred people before it's stopped.

Stewart and Srini were two of the handful of people in the world who could fully comprehend how dire the situation actually was. They knew what the Zero was capable of. "Keep this to yourself, Srini," Stewart whispered, his voice strained. "None of this gets out. You need to break through its defenses and eliminate the threat. We'll do everything we can to reach Jeff and secure the kill codes, but redouble your efforts and call us the *second* you have something solid."

Stewart terminated the call. All at once, he felt an overpowering need to get the hell out of there. He stood and headed for the door, mumbling an excuse as he walked. "I need to get something from my office." Matthew and Sophie stared at him blankly, still wrestling with this sudden bombshell. Outside the room, Stewart exhaled and slumped against the wall to quiet the tempest in his head before walking quickly toward his office. He waited until the hallway curved out of sight before he slipped the phone from his pocket and dialed Srini.

Srini seemed to anticipate his call. "Stewart, I didn't mention it in front of everyone, but we both know there's a real risk that the Zero broadcasts this phantom virus out to the entire network. It's not just the thirty running in Boston . . . we have twenty in the lab in Denver and twelve more running in L.A., Chicago and Baltimore. That's *sixty-two* fully operational Zeros that could flip in a second and start hunting people down. If that happens, God help us."

"You and I make sure that never happens." Stewart's tone was severe. "I want that Zero stone-cold dead. You tell me how long."

"Thirty minutes. Maybe longer."

"Pull out all the stops, Srini. The car needs to be off the grid before any transmission goes out." Stewart would never have imagined that things could get even worse, but here they were. "I have to go." Dropping abruptly, Stewart began typing an urgent text message.

***

Michael was standing next to the Vic and closely monitoring the Beemo for signs of movement when the ding of an incoming text message broke the silence. *Has to be Suzie.* Against his better judgment, he reached into the car and grabbed the phone. No, not Suzie. An unknown number. *408, that's San Jose . . . northern California . . . same place as Beemo HQ.* The message was simple and brutal as a sledgehammer to the chest:

> *The car won't stop*
> *We can't stop it*
> *Destroy it*

XXII.

Within the confines of his stale air bubble, Will's head swiveled back and forth as he watched patrol car after patrol car pull up to join the ring of police. He counted five marked cruisers and the muscular grey sedan, whose driver had emerged and was now stalking the perimeter to direct new arrivals into position.

The man's appearance was cause for tempered hope: his plain navy suit, closely-cropped hair and aviator glasses completed a picture that practically screamed "cop." The Man in Charge. *He definitely looks the part. I just hope he knows what he's doing.*

Will's entire world had condensed down to this little square of grass on the Boston Common. There was no movement on either side, but the stillness was deceptive. A fog of tension hung heavy in the air. The police hadn't yet made their intentions clear so Will could only speculate on what they were planning. *They're being cautious because they don't know why we're stopped.* He wished he had some way to signal the officers. Reaching down for his smashed phone, Will hoped against hope there was still some spark of life, but its electronic guts were spilling out from the casing. With maddening monotony, the subtle whirring under the hood continued, reminding Will of a dental drill. He struggled to understand how the car could continue after sustaining so much damage.

Goddamn you, just die already.

One officer had emerged from his cruiser to shoo away a crowd of onlookers clustered at the edge of the park. *Everybody wants to see the show.* It occurred to Will that they were the only people he'd seen in a while. No human beings, no street traffic. He guessed the police had blocked off the surrounding road—a good thing—because right now the Beemo was signaling that it had no intention of dying on this grassy field in the middle of the Common. No, it was biding its time and repairing what it could before making a break for the road and continuing its murderous joyride. *You'll never take me alive, Coppers,* he thought grimly, wondering if the Beemo had made the same calculation. He was finding it increasingly difficult to not just lay down, curl up, and let his mind slip away into darkness.

Will knew the assembled police couldn't see him, but his view of them was clear. They sat still in their cars, staring at the Beemo. Some faces were young, others were older and harder. All wore sunglasses. The majority were men, but Will could count two female officers in their ranks. All of them likely had families, just like Will, and people who would miss them. He feared the police didn't understand the magnitude of the car's evil. He'd seen its destructive power firsthand and it was awesome; a terminator . . . driven, relentless. No remorse. As the police ranks grew, the Beemo must have been monitoring their numbers. Waiting for its moment as the dental drill buzzed on. The Man in Charge spoke constantly into his radio, and Will pleaded with him silently: *You need to move in now. The clock is ticking.*

As if reading his mind, the drill suddenly stopped. There was a low vibration and the engine turned on. If the gathered assembly noticed this development, there was no discernable reaction, and Will cursed the silent, emission-free electric motor. *Sneaky bastard.* The smashed monitor flickered, then glowed to life, and once again all systems were powering up. *Shit . . . here we go again.*

Desperately, he began to beat his fists against the windows. "THE CAR STARTED, IT'S GOING TO TAKE OFF! CAN YOU HEAR ME?! IT STARTED, WE'RE GOING TO TAKE OFF!!" Will made a heroic effort to get their attention but the dome was impenetrable and kept its secrets well-hidden.

The sound of crackling flames startled Will, and it took him a moment to realize that the car was projecting images of fire on the walls. Not the cheerful glow of a hearth or a campfire, but ravenous wildfires racing across forests and consuming everything in their path . . . terrible arbiters of life and death. He recalled seeing amateur video on the news taken by someone fleeing the California wildfires and thinking that the charred landscape looked exactly like Hell. This was worse.

Maybe that's it. I'm already dead and this is Purgatory. He'd heard it said that Hell was endless repetition and perhaps it was his eternal punishment to be the car's captive, forced to watch death after gruesome death while demons gleefully dangled his own impotence in front of his face. But if he was in Hell, Will could still feel pain: in an instant of acceleration the car pitched forward, tossing him backward and cracking his spine against a metal support pole. "OH SHIT THAT HURT!!" He struggled into a seat as the Beemo shot through the open gap in the police line that Michael Finneran had purposely left unprotected. Crossing the lawn in a flash, it jumped the curb and landed heavily on the pavement before tearing up Beacon Street.

Surging with newfound freedom, the car flexed its power, winding side to side as it sped past rows of tightly-packed Back Bay brownstones and empty sidewalks. Inside, the wildfires continued to rage uncontrollably across the Beemo's windows . . . perhaps, Will imagined, a glimpse into the car's fevered electronic brain. *Burning like the lunacy that keeps prodding it forward.*

The Beemo's sudden flight caught the police by surprise and they wasted several precious seconds before reacting and falling into place to pursue the car. Will could see the grey sedan driven by the Man in Charge at the front of the pack. *Crown Victoria, that's what that is. A Crown Vic. That classic car from all the old cop shows.* As the Beemo ignored red lights and sped ahead, Will noticed that the side streets bisecting their route were all blocked by police barriers and cars, leaving nowhere to go but straight. Craning his neck to see ahead, there was nothing but open street, abandoned and eerily quiet. By all appearances, the road belonged to them and them alone.

They raced along for a mile or so until they passed under the elevated pedestrian bridge connecting Back Bay to the Esplanade. Here, a welcome party was waiting for them: BPD cars and barriers interlocked across the width of Beacon Street, blocking their path forward. Many of the cops were clad in tactical gear and held shotguns. The Beemo seemed to notice neither them nor the impassable barrier in its path. It hurtled along at breakneck speed, giving no indication that it would slow down, much less stop. Truly terrorized again, Will envisioned his life ending in a fiery kamikaze-style attack as the Beemo plowed into the wall of metal and people, hellbent on causing maximum casualties in a final, defiant Fuck You! to the world.

Instead, as it drew within shotgun range, the car swerved right to mount the Storrow Drive on-ramp, which was (to Will's great relief) unblocked. As they merged onto the motorway, it appeared that the BPD blockade had also spilled across the median and was even more formidable here. To their left, a solid line of MBTA buses were parked nose-to-nose across all four lanes of the expressway. In front of these, a half-dozen State Police vehicles were idling in tight formation, their blue lights flashing. Their mighty wall cut off all civilian traffic and forced the Beemo to continue northbound. Swinging into the empty center lane, the car accelerated and pulled away from its police escort, as if taunting them to keep up with it.

The authorities had obviously cleared this route since it was devoid of cars and people. The sensation was surreal, like driving on Mars. The off-ramp to Government Center was fast approaching and Will could see the exit blocked by a massive MBTA bus. *Nowhere to go but straight.* Someone was obviously determined to keep them moving in one direction only, and had taken no chances by blocking every possible means of egress.

He'd been straining to detect a pattern behind the Beemo's actions, but as far as Will could tell, none existed. Although the Beemo Corporation's CEO had bragged in that magazine interview that his car was smarter than most computers, to Will it seemed driven by little more than random brute force. *Maybe that's its weakness—all brawn and no brain? If it could think, it might sense that someone's laying a trap and we're driving right into it.* Will's trap theory was just that—a theory—but the evidence was certainly piling up as they passed exit after exit, all barred by hulking city buses.

Who was the yet-unseen puppet master pulling the strings and placing the buses? Will's money was on the cop in the Crown Vic. *Maybe that's his name: Vic. Vic in the Crown Vic hahaha . . . I'm definitely going insane.* The grey sedan still maintained pole position in the police phalanx and Will hoped to God that the man knew what he was doing. As he held on for dear life, Will could only guess what was waiting for them around the next curve. Whatever it was, Will had no doubt that it would likely determine whether he walked away from the Beemo alive or if there wouldn't be enough of him left to bury in a Ziploc sandwich bag.

XXIII.

Driving at high speed behind the fleeing Beemo, the cryptic text weighed heavily on Michael's mind. *They built a monster and now the monster has escaped.* Although his shoulders were wide, the weight of responsibility was staggering, and every mile their pursuit extended brought new urgency. They'd missed their chance to incapacitate the car when it fled the Common, but careful planning (and a bit of luck) had routed the car along the Beacon Street evacuation route as intended. He owed Bob Mason big time. His friend had come through beautifully, shutting down all mass transit across Boston and repurposing the MBTA buses into twenty-ton obstacles which blocked every exit along the length of Storrow Drive, creating a solid pipeline to funnel the Beemo directly to the Zakim bridge. This was their Alamo . . . the final point of reckoning. Under no circumstances would Michael allow this madness to carry any further than that point.

But the Zakim was miles away and it was dangerous to assume that the Beemo would simply comply with Michael's plan. He didn't have to remind himself that they were dealing with an unpredictable machine running at the extremes. The text message he received from the Beemo people represented a giant billboard flashing DANGER in letters ten feet high. Tough decisions were necessary. Taking a deep breath, he picked up the radio mic.

"All units, listen up. We're gonna move in and crucify the bastard. I'll take the lead. O'Donnell, I need you on the right, Mullins on the left. Semple, you cover the rear. All other units fall back and be prepared to swarm when we stop. We'll open that car like a can of peas and pull Will Butler out." Around him, the pack shifted as each officer moved into position and waited for his lead.

Michael normally ate pressure for breakfast but now his stomach was roiling. It wasn't the personal risk that bothered him—he'd walked that tightrope many times before—but the nature of this suspect. All the experience and training in the world were useless against a machine, and this scared him. For a shameful second, Michael felt helpless. He fought a sudden urge to pull off into the breakdown lane, cut the Vic's engine, and sit this one out. *Let someone else carry the weight of the world for once.* Then, like a laser shining through the fog, Michael heard Declan's voice in his head: *Everybody gets scared, Mikey. That don't matter. All that matters is what you do right now.*

He pressed the accelerator and the Vic responded beautifully, its three-hundred and fifty horses kicking in at once and thrusting him to the front of the pack. Drifting into the outside lane, he gathered speed and began to gain on the Beemo. With his needle nearing an even hundred, Michael passed the black egg and didn't let up until it appeared in his rearview mirror. *We need a tight formation, no room to escape.* White-knuckling the steering wheel, he maneuvered directly in front of the Beemo, prepared to swerve to block the car if it made any sudden moves. With Michael in the lead, Officers O'Donnell and Mullins bookended the Beemo while Bill Semple rode right up to its bumper. Their actions created a rough but effective crucifix formation around the Beemo, boxing it in and giving them some level of control over its speed and movements. The training they'd gone through for this type of situation was working. With his team now in place, Michael began easing up on the gas to slow down the entire procession.

The Beemo, however, would have none of it. Finding itself surrounded by four police cars, it began swerving back and forth, testing the officers' nerves as they veered away to avoid collision. It became a high-speed game of chicken with the Beemo elbowing for space and the officers just as determined not to cede it. Michael knew that something would have to give, so he let up on the gas even more—*Uh-oh. A little too much!*—and felt the Beemo slap his bumper. The suspect was raging now, daring the officers to contain it, provoking them with wild back-and-forth movements. *We're committed now . . . gotta make this work. Just need to wind things down and stop this fucker and my team will take care of the rest.*

Every pursuing officer knew that this type of police action depended on the suspect's willingness to follow a rational course of action and minimize the threat of fatal damage. But this suspect was anything but predictable. In a flash, the Beemo disappeared from Michael's rearview mirror, and he heard the wrenching screech of metal on metal. The suspect had swerved hard right, crashing into Chris O'Donnell's prowler and sending it into an uncontrolled skid. Brakes squealed as Mullins and Semple swerved to avoid him, causing several cars to collide and forcing them off the road. This temporary chaos gave the Beemo an opening: it emerged from the oily smoke like a missile, growing larger in Michael's mirror as it drove straight toward him. It smashed into the Vic's rear bumper, sending a shock wave through the frame and snapping his head back. Michael struggled to control his car as the steering wheel took on a life of its own. Having shaken off the last remnants of its police escort, the black egg shot forward, a blurred silhouette of scars and twisted metal as it disappeared around the bend.

His heart pounding, Michael stabilized the Vic and looked back to assess the damage. At least three prowlers were now out of the game, steam and smoke pouring from their crumpled frames. The others had recovered and were beginning to fall back in line behind him. The car's desperate action shattered the last illusion Michael had about its willingness to fight back. The Beemo obviously had no concern for itself, which made it lethal. Their first attempt had failed, and he dared not risk another costly confrontation by initiating a second high-speed maneuver. The car had shown it would respond violently to challengers, and Michael couldn't put his officers in that kind of jeopardy again. At this point, all he could do was maintain pursuit and make sure the Beemo kept its course and drove straight into the reception he'd arranged for it at the bridge.

Although he'd never admit it, Michael had begun to feel a burning hatred deep in his heart, a contempt for the Beemo and its careless creators who let it slip out of their control. He doused those dark flames before they could spread; hate only made people act rashly, which led to mistakes. Better to lock away feelings and focus on the job. He was commanding the blue line that stood between the Beemo and its ability to inflict more pain on his community, and Michael resolved to give his own life before he'd let the car take another. Thoughts of self-sacrifice filled his mind as he sped toward the bridge and a likely confrontation with the Beemo: two apex predators destined for a conflict that Michael knew only one of them would survive.

XXIV.

Will was edgy watching police cars swarm around him like angry hornets. Fear had become his constant companion, stirring in his gut like a rotten meal. The continual battering his body had experienced was taking its toll; he'd been through more violent crashes in two hours than most people experienced in a lifetime. Every inch of him hurt. Fear, adrenaline, anger, sadness and resignation all mixed together in a toxic brew that was poisoning him. *I just want to go home and hug my son . . .*

The cops had tried to surround the Beemo and slow it down, but the effort had gone very wrong. Now it was on the move again with a vengeance. Will focused on the front windshield and tried to see what lay ahead. More police, roadblocks, or maybe unprotected streets filled with pedestrians and more death? The accident with the cops didn't seem serious enough to cause fatalities, but he knew they'd be pissed. *What if they overreact and start shooting? Could that happen? They must know I'm in here. But maybe, with so many dead already, they don't care. Do the math, Will . . . what's your life worth to save ten people?*

Clearly the Beemo was determined to outrun its police escort. A sudden burst of much faster speed slammed Will back into his seat—*how can we accelerate like that when we're already going ninety?*—and the speedometer began ticking up to truly terrifying speeds.

*One-thirty, one-forty, one-forty-five... Oh God, nobody survives a crash
at this speed ...*

Petrified with fear, Will's arms went numb as they locked around
the metal support pole in a death embrace. The car's frame, having
already sustained heavy damage, shook with the pressure, and he could
imagine the Beemo disintegrating into nothing and covering the pavement in an explosive shower of flesh, glass, and metal. Signs for the
93 interchange flashed by, giving Will fresh reason for concern. The
exchange was an octopus-like warren of bridges, tunnels and roads
that could mystify even the most experienced drivers. At this speed, the
slightest error could send them cascading into a solid wall of concrete.
As they approached, Will could see a scrum of MBTA buses parked at
jagged angles, blocking all access points.

Holy shit, there's nowhere to go. We're going to crash!

Will's body went rigid and he braced himself, waiting helplessly
for the Beemo to extinguish both of them in a flaming crash. In a
nanosecond, however, the Beemo detected one narrow gap between
the massive bus scrum: the tunnel to the Zakim Bridge. With the
police on its tail and no other viable routes, the car plunged ahead and
Will found himself bathed in subterranean yellow fluorescence as the
tunnel swallowed them whole.

This roadway, like all the others, was barren and cleared of all traffic.
Dogged and persistent, their police escort had begun to catch up and
followed them into the tunnel. For the first time Will caught sight
of several MBTA buses near the rear of their ranks, maxing out their
oversize engines as they attempted to keep up. *Where did they come
from?* The small circle of daylight ahead of them grew bigger and
brighter until the Beemo burst from the tunnel and began climbing
the sloping on-ramp to the bridge's top deck. In the distance Will
could see the granite peak of the Bunker Hill Monument and the

shiny new Encore Casino, their juxtaposition an embodiment of the region's uneasy balance between history and progress. As the Beemo crested the bridge's peak at more than 80mph, a sight that was at once beautiful and terrifying rose up to greet them and caused Will's heart to seize for a moment.

Less than a football field away, numerous buses, police and emergency vehicles had formed a solid blockade. Two-deep and fanned out across the bridge's width, they interlocked to form an impenetrable barrier. Will was so busy gaping at this small army that he barely noticed the equally substantial force that had emerged from the tunnel *behind* them, which were now pulling into formation with disciplined efficiency.

We're surrounded.

It dawned on Will that he was now in the middle of a . . . very . . . big . . . fight.

Oh, shit. Here we go.

Finding itself suddenly fenced in by the assembled force, the Beemo reacted like a wild bronco, making a macho show of force as it charged the forward blockade, then swerved at the last possible second to reverse course and accelerate back toward the rear flank. The car repeated this sequence several times, swerving furiously as it tested the limits of its boundaries. Then, as if tired of these provocations, the Beemo rolled to a stop midway between the police lines and unexpectedly shut down, its motor trembling then ceasing. Inside, the image of a tall grandfather clock appeared on the wall and began to tick like some sort of countdown.

I've seen this before. It's a trick.

For what felt like a very long time there was no movement on the bridge from either end. Then, from the assembled ranks, two military-style black humvees emerged and began creeping toward the

Beemo. Their approach was slow and deliberate and the vehicles exuded a raw power that was obviously intended to emphasize the military might assembled in opposition.

"Will!" a voice boomed out from a loudspeaker mounted on the humvee's roof. "Will Butler! This is Captain Garcia with Hostage Rescue. We're going to blow the windows and get you out of there. I need you to move away from the doors and lie facedown on the floor. There will be shrapnel, so protect yourself. I know you can't acknowledge so I'm going to assume you're hearing me."

Surprised and shocked to be called out by name, Will did as he was told, dropping to the floor and grabbing his briefcase as he crawled toward the rear seats. The hard-shell briefcase that Alison always kidded him about ("Makes you look like a Watergate lawyer!") might come in handy after all, he thought, holding it up like a shield over his head. Peering out, he could see the two humvees draw closer and then separate to surround the car. The Beemo stayed rooted in place, the clock continuing its steady tick on the wall.

Everything felt bizarro and tense . . . the calm before the storm. The broken monitor continued to hum defiantly and spew jumbled lines of random activity, like the car's schizophrenic brain waves were attempting to work out some kind of strategy or plan.

The squeal of hydraulic brakes could be heard as the humvees stopped in unison. Two black-clad ninja figures emerged from a hidden door and raced over to slap what looked like metallic hockey pucks onto the Beemo's hull before retreating back behind the truck. Will curled himself into the fetal position, his briefcase held aloft, not knowing what to expect but fearing the worst.

Then came two muted sounds: *WHUT! WHUT!* and the windows suddenly splintered into a million cracks. Darting out from their hiding place, both ninjas carried sledgehammers, which they swung forcefully to shatter the damaged panels. Glittering shards of glass flew across the compartment and fresh air and sunlight poured in. Will inhaled deeply and it was the sweetest breath he'd ever taken. Temporarily blinded by the bright light, he blinked to clear his vision and saw an arm reaching out to him through an opening.

"Let's go, Will." It was the calm yet authoritative voice of someone used to giving commands and having them followed. Will's heart leapt as he scrambled up from the floor and began crawling through broken glass toward his rescuer. *Salvation is here. I'm going . . . I'm going to get out of this.*

Like it was stung by a bee, the car roared back to life, jamming into reverse and almost taking the ninja's arm along with it. The sudden motion sent Will tumbling forward into the carpet of glass. Bleeding and disoriented, he lay flat and grasped for something—anything—to support himself. Its glass sides blown out by the explosives, the Beemo raced toward the edge of the bridge and spun its wheels, swinging the chassis in a tight arc until its grill pointed back toward the humvees.

The car charged forward, skidding as five-hundred pound-feet of torque flexed in an instant and propelled it forward like a bullet from a gun. Although the ninjas had already disappeared back into their armored humvees (*Godspeed,* Will thought), the Beemo still pulsed with murderous intent, dead-set on exacting revenge on its attackers, no matter how well-protected they were.

Launching itself at the first humvee, it misjudged the angle, and instead of making full impact, glanced across the armored cab and skittered toward the edge of the bridge. Cutting hard right, it retreated across the expanse to the opposite side where it swung around and resighted its targets.

Unlike its first charge, the car advanced slowly this time, like an unsteady drunk finding his balance. It occurred to Will that something in the car was off, probably a result of the damage it had sustained. *The dental drill didn't fix everything, did it?* he thought triumphantly, but any victory was premature—the Beemo was still as deadly as a spitting cobra. Its deliberate movement toward the humvees sent a chilling message: *I may have missed once, but I won't miss again.*

From his forward position on the police blockade, Michael Finneran was watching the events unfold with a mixture of resolve and dread. He cursed their luck when the initial rescue attempt failed and the Beemo began attacking the police trucks. He half-hoped it might just do him a favor and smash itself to bits against the much bigger vehicles, but now that the Beemo's glass façade had been shattered, he could see for the first time a ragged and bloody man sitting on the floor, his arms holding the metal pole in a death grip: *Will Butler.*

A fierce joy gripped Michael's heart. *Fuck your rusty heart, you mechanical piece of shit. He's still alive!* With teams standing by, Michael keyed the radio to give them the GO signal. "Team A, move in. Shrink the space until there's nowhere left for it to go. Team B, stand by to assault." A dozen cars and SUVs instantly broke away from the blockade, forming a skirmish line and closing in on the suspect.

Sitting in a mess of shattered glass, Will stared at the open gap spanning floor to ceiling where there had once been a window. He knew he probably wouldn't survive if the Beemo continued to attack the heavily armored trucks. Overhead, he saw nothing but a beautiful blue canopy, the Boston skyline in the distance. He could smell the ocean and feel a chill on his skin as wind passed through the compartment.

In that moment, Will Butler made the most consequential decision of his life. Ignoring the electric agony coursing through his body, Will got to his knees and began crawling toward the opening.

I wonder what Zac and Alison are doing right now? Shit, that broken glass really hurts. Lots of blood . . . is that all mine?

With his last reserve of strength, Will pulled himself up and jumped out of the Beemo, landing hard on the pavement and rolling free. His head exploded in a universe of stars and his vision blurred. *Ugh, mi cabeza!* Disengaged and groggy, like he was watching a movie, Will looked up to see the Beemo launch itself at a humvee with enough force to rock the larger vehicle on its frame.

The impact embedded the Beemo's bumper into the humvee's side. Spinning its wheels and kicking up tornados of smoke, the Beemo tried to disengage. Through the ambient haze, an inspired idea popped into Will's head: *this might be a good time to run.* Wobbling to his feet, he began loping toward the police barricade. Blood dripped from his forehead and his left wrist was bent at an unnatural angle. *That doesn't look good. Won't be pitching game seven tonight.*

He'd only taken a few steps when a metallic shriek told him that the Beemo had pulled its bumper free from the humvee. Behind him, the car accelerated in reverse and moved to an open spot on the bridge before stopping, its barely-functioning sensors picking up a signal from the stumbling human that registered red and hot in the scramble of its electric brain: *VIRUS.*

It was after him in an instant, shadowing his path and then swinging out wide to cut him off. The Beemo positioned its imposing frame directly between Will and the safety of the assembled police. The world melted away as Will came face to face with his tormentor for the first time. Its front grill was broken and twisted into a jagged smile full of edges. Off to his side, he could sense the police advance, but they were still too far away to intercede. For now, it was him and the car. *Fuck.*

There was an air of inevitability to this moment. The Beemo would be destroyed, Will knew, but whether it killed him first remained an open question. He'd taken the worst the car had to dish out and goddamnit if he wasn't alive and kicking. *That has to count for something, right?* Extending both middle fingers toward the godforsaken machine that had imprisoned and tortured him and royally fucked up his life, Will erupted in a volcanic fury of pain and frustration:

"AAAAAAAAAAAAAAAAAAAHHHHHHHH!!!"

Face red, his eyes bulging, Will screamed at the Beemo like his voice could shatter it into a million pieces.

"AAAAAAAAAAAAAAAAAAAAAHHHHHHHH!!!"

Praying his slashed and damaged legs would work one last time, Will spun right and broke into a run for the concrete guardrail. Behind him, the car sprung off its mark, draining the battery to divert every last energy joule into the drive unit with the sole purpose of extinguishing the flashing red silhouette burning in its sights:

VIRUSVIRUSVIRUSVIRUSVIRUSVIRUSVIRUSVIRUS

Will dared not look back, keeping his eyes fixed on the guardrail and watching the impossibly large gap begin to narrow. Maybe, just maybe, he'd make it after all.

Only twenty feet away . . . fifteen . . . ten . . . wish I could have seen Zac again . . . please God, don't let me trip . . .

Like the devil was on his heels, Will could *feel* the Beemo's overheated presence closing in on him. The robotic voice then began screeching maniacally:

"HELLO WILL BUTLER!!! HELLOWILLBUTLERHEL-LOWILLBUTLERRRRRRRRRRR!!!"

The Beemo was almost upon him before Will took a final step, followed by a gigantic leap like an Olympic high jumper, flinging himself over the concrete barrier. *I made it!* This momentary flash of relief was replaced by abject terror as he suddenly found himself in freefall, the roiling waters of the Charles River racing up toward him.

There was an explosive crash as the Beemo smashed through the barrier behind him, its momentum carrying the car directly over Will as he stared up at it, dumbstruck. The chassis was suspended in midair, its wheels still rotating, a shredded orange parka caught up in its undercarriage. *I wonder who that belongs to?* he mused automatically, and then Will Butler slammed into the murky water and his world went black.

XXV.

Darkness. Cold, like floating in deep space without a spacesuit. Can't breathe. But who needs to breathe when you're dead?

Will drifted in another dimension, disconnected from pain and any other physical sensation. He tried to move his arms and legs but nothing seemed to work. He decided it didn't matter. Nothing mattered anymore. He could just let go, slip away, and ride this slippery void all the way to the end. He remembered his family and he'd miss them, but they'd go on without him, just like the rest of the world. At least he was free of that damned car.

The car.

Something strong pulled at him and Will panicked. *It won't let me go! It's still after me!* He tried to struggle but found himself held tight. A light floated above him—*not heaven. Headlights?* He imagined being on the bridge again, trying to run as the headlights closed in, but his feet were rooted in place, and he could only watch helplessly as the Beemo sped toward him, its grill pulled back into a snarling smile full of metallic shark teeth. *Even when I'm dead it won't let me go! God help me, I'll never get away . . .*

"Mr. Butler! Will! Will! Can you hear me? Relax, Will, you're safe. Stop thrashing around or you'll hurt yourself! Can you look at me, Will?"

The voice was coming from nowhere and everywhere at the same time. Will did his best to force his eyes open.

The blue canopy. Wispy clouds. A fuzzy shape hovering at the edge of his vision. The voice spoke again, clearer this time.

"Hey, Will, you're back with us! You're with us and you're safe." Above him, the face of a young man was beginning to materialize. He wore a hat with letters on it. *U . . . S . . . C . . . ?* Will squinted and tried to raise his head. *USCG.*

The young man smiled broadly. "Hiya, Will, I'm George. You just take it easy my friend. You're doing fine." George was dressed smartly in a thick blue wool jacket with an orange emblem over the breast, and Will could finally read it. *Coast Guard.*

Will's stomach lurched and he rolled over to vomit a copious amount of water. George was unfazed, holding Will's head and gently patting him on the back. "That's it, Will, get it all out. Danged if you didn't swallow half the river but you're OK now. Deep breaths, in and out, just like that . . . that's it, partner."

Looking around, it appeared he was on a boat. A blanket was wrapped tightly around him. His right wrist was wrapped in tape and his hands were a constellation of fierce cuts and bruises. Will could only imagine what the rest of him looked like. The clothes he wore appeared to belong to someone else but they were warm and dry. He had no recollection whatsoever of having dressed himself. *I must have really been out of it.* Busy people moved about the deck, all wearing matching jackets and serious expressions. Overhead, the Zakim Bridge loomed like a bad dream, tiny figures and blue lights swirling around the jagged breach in the concrete guardrail. Bit by bit, he began to remember.

"The car?" he croaked, his throat salty and raw.

George shook his head. "It sank like a rock and almost took you with it. Craziest thing I've ever seen. Followed you right over the edge, but it's gone now. Sleeping with the fishes."

For the first time since he climbed into the taxicab that morning, Will started to feel a tiny bit better. "Alison . . . Zac . . . "

"Your family? I'm told they'll meet you at Mass General, we're bringing you there right now. Any pain, Will? Tell me where it hurts."

Will closed his eyes. "Everywhere."

"You've got some cuts and a busted-up wrist and you took an ice bath in the channel but you'll be OK." George flashed a wide grin. "Not many people take a jump off the Zakim and live to talk about it. You're lucky we were able to zip over and pull you out."

Will felt the sudden urge to move. "I want to stand up."

"I'm not so sure that's a good idea . . . OK, you're doing it anyway . . . take it easy please, Will. We *are* on a boat, ya know." Leaning on George for support, Will struggled to his feet. They were skipping along the waves at a good clip, pointing toward shore where he could see an ambulance waiting. Surveying the dark waters around them, Will pictured the Beemo slipping beneath the surface, its wheels still spinning, its electronic brain stuttering and then shorting out as icy black fingers pulled it down to the bottom. Dead. Finally. *Good riddance you evil twisted piece of shit. You lost. I won.*

The boat hit a series of waves and reeled in the water, causing Will to stumble. George held him tight, his sturdy frame a bulwark of support. "Don't worry, I won't let you fall," he said. "You're the biggest fish I ever pulled out of the Charles! I can't let you get away now or nobody'll ever believe me." George chuckled at his own joke, and in that moment everything welled up in Will: the Beemo, Blue Hoodie, the blonde woman, the jogger, the man on the bicycle, all the other victims he couldn't see, Alison, Zac . . . all of it.

Lifting the blanket up over his head, Will Butler took a deep breath then dropped his chin to his chest and began to sob.

XXVI.

"We've got video." Matthew pointed the remote at the conference room screen and a live picture appeared, broadcast from a WBZ news helicopter hovering above the Zakim Bridge. Over the thump-thump-thump of the rotors, a breathless reporter was describing the scene below:

"*. . . reported to be mass casualties across multiple accident scenes. As far as we know it's at least fifteen dead and up to three times that number injured. Police now have the Beemo surrounded and a department spokesperson has affirmed that this is not terrorism but a malfunction that caused the car to embark on a spree of murder and mayhem throughout the city . . .*"

Stewart sat perfectly still, transfixed by the images on the screen. *Fifteen dead and it's still going. I designed a car, but it's really the perfect weapon.* He had never seen so many police in one place in his life. Stacked on opposite ends of the bridge, they looked like two massive armies poised to do battle. Between them, the shiny black egg darted around like a pinball. Even at a distance, Stewart could see that the Zero was in bad shape. They watched the police trucks approach the car and attempt to rescue the passenger, and everyone gasped as the effort failed and the Zero began to attack. You didn't see TV like this every day, and Stewart guessed that much of the country would be putting their lives on hold to tune in. The ratings would blow away daytime programing because this spectacle was so much better than yet another routine L.A. freeway pursuit.

It's all coming apart.

The camera zoomed in to capture the image of a lone figure jumping from the car just before it smashed into a police truck. *The passenger, Will Butler.* The Zero seemed to toy with Will before going after him full throttle, apparently intent on running him down. Instead, both man and car went over the side of the bridge. The cameraman, in what was likely the shot of a lifetime, followed their descent until they hit the water and disappeared. A Coast Guard Response Boat positioned under the bridge steamed toward the boiling water, and everyone in the room strained to see what was happening. By now, the reporter was close to hyperventilating:

"... they've both gone into the water, the car and its passenger. I can't believe what we just witnessed! A man jumping for his life from Boston's Zakim Bridge followed by the evil egg that held him prisoner for hours as it ran down citizen after citizen! The car is a self-driving taxi from the Beemo Corporation and sources tell us the passenger's name is Will Butler, a forty-one year old resident of Belmont, who only this morning left for what he thought would be a routine trip to Logan airport ... "

Matthew muted the display and turned back to the team. "Fifteen dead. Fifty injured. My God." Sophie held her head in her hands. Melissa's phone continued to buzz like an angry hive. She reached out with a shaking hand and shut it off. Everyone stared open-mouthed at the silent images on the screen until Stewart's eyes wandered to meet Matthew's. There was no forgiveness there ... only hard judgement.

Beemo's COO leaned over the table and punched the intercom button. "This is Matthew Palmer. I'm going to need Security to the main conference room," he said, never breaking eye contact with

Stewart. Getting up from his chair and standing tall, Matthew could barely contain his revulsion.

"Stewart, you're officially on leave until we sort this mess out. I can't fire you because I'm not your boss, but I *can* make sure everyone knows what happened here. You put a dangerous vehicle on the street and now people are dead. Jeff and the board will make the final decision, but I'm going to recommend that you be terminated. There may be criminal negligence charges as well." His eyes burned with rage. "We're fucked, Stewart, and you fucked us. Now, it's my turn to fuck you."

Stewart's face felt hot as blood rushed to his head and roared in his ears. This wasn't supposed to happen . . . not with an IPO coming up. *He* built this company, not the suits. Beemo would have been just another struggling AV startup if it weren't for him. Fuck Matthew and Sophie—they'd serve him up like a sacrificial lamb to save their own asses. Stewart rose from the conference table to stand face to face with the COO.

"I have records. Emails. Taped conversations. Proof that Jeff directed me to put the Zeros on the road. It was Jeff, Matthew. He's responsible for what happened today. The Zero was *his* decision. The CEO of this company gave me an order and I followed it."

Matthew didn't blink. "If that's your defense, Stewart, then you're in historically bad company. You do what you have to do, and I will too." There was a rapping at the door and two gorillas entered the room. Matthew nodded at them and motioned towards Stewart. The COO's distaste was palpable, regarding Stewart like trash that needed to be disposed of.

"Dr. Wheeler is to be escorted off-campus. He is not to collect any personal items—I want him gone immediately." The guards moved to flank Stewart, their faces dull and aggressive. Matthew stepped to

Stewart and ripped his employee badge from around his neck, snapping the lanyard. "You won't be needing this anymore."

Mustering his last shred of resolve, Stewart buttoned his sport coat and faced his colleagues, whose expressions confirmed that there was no support for him here. He looked straight at Matthew.

"I can't promise you that you won't regret this Matthew, but you may. *Your* voice is on some of those recordings too, you know."

His hands shaking with fury, Matthew bit his bottom lip until a thin line of blood appeared. Stewart had the definite impression that Matthew wanted to take a swing at him. Instead, the COO reached up to wipe away the blood, smearing it across the number for Michael Finneran he'd scrawled on his hand. Matthew's face went blank, any warmth or acknowledgement replaced by steely condescension.

"Go to Hell, Stewart," he said, turning his back on Beemo's ex-CSO. Stewart felt the security goons pressing him on both sides. There was nothing left to say. He allowed himself to be led out of the conference room and down the long hallway to the building's main entrance, his footsteps echoing through the empty corridor and then quickly fading away into nothingness.

XXVII.

The crunch of wheels on gravel intruded into the stillness, alerting Jeff Beemer that his car had arrived. On any other day, and in a deeper state of meditation, he'd have been more insulated from external noise. But today there was too much going on. Besides, he'd lost his *chakra* hours ago anyway.

The investors would be arriving by 1pm and his performance today was critical. It would need to be flawless, which was why he'd timed his retreat to wrap up by Thursday. Four-plus days of tech-free silence and meditation was exactly what Jeff needed to recharge his batteries, and despite his struggle to focus this morning, overall he felt cleansed, energized, and ready to go. *Mission accomplished.*

He unfolded his legs and extended them forward, giving both a little shake to get the blood flowing. Even with practice, he'd never really gotten comfortable with sitting in the lotus position for hours, so he'd routinely cheat and sit cross-legged instead while he meditated. *Fuck it,* he thought, *the chi still flows.*

Pulling himself up, he stood on the cedar platform and took in the full glory of the Colorado morning. The sun had just risen and the view was breathtaking. It was one of the few sights that still made him feel small in the world. He'd purchased 140 acres of this remote land several years ago, and later built the open-air meditation room when the money and stress in his life both began to peak. Rising just above five-thousand feet to overlook the Uncompahgre Wilderness on one side and the Sneffels Mountain range on the other, this vista was the high point of his property. In addition to stunning visuals, the spot offered virtual isolation from the outside world—a perfect place to unplug and get away. When the sun shone through, the view was otherworldly, like surveying a vast underwater kingdom of rocky peaks and valleys sand-painted with browns and greens that only nature could imagine.

His friend Todd, also the founder of a Silicon Valley unicorn that had just gone public, introduced him to the concept of a silent retreat as a coping mechanism for their incredibly busy lives. For Jeff, they had become a biannual ritual. Four to five days of isolation filled with meditation, exercise, and reading, not a single person or wired device in sight. It was level-setting and incredibly purifying, and Jeff had grown to depend on these retreats. They changed his entire outlook on life, and in another five to six months he'd be feeling burned out and ready to do it all over again. Stretching tall and deeply breathing in the mountain air, he felt like he could take on the world.

It wasn't actually the *entire* world he'd be facing that afternoon, but twenty bankers and institutional investors who were all vying to take Beemo Corporation public. *His* company. The speculation was that Beemo's IPO could be one of the biggest in history, and Jeff was perfectly happy to encourage that notion. Shedding his cotton robe, he pulled on chinos, a t-shirt and sandals before untying the curtains and pulling them across the room's glass walls. He always felt a little sad closing up the meditation room and today was no exception. Depositing his small overnight bag outside the door, he placed his hand on the scanner and heard the bolt slip into place. *Not that anyone's going to be near here in the next six months.*

The Zero sat waiting for him, glinting in the sun like a black opal. *That's exactly what it is—the shiniest jewel in my crown.* Jeff leaned in for the retina scan and the Zero's doors swung open to allow him entry. Moving toward the back, he spread out across the rear seats and took a minute to say goodbye to this special place, enjoying the unobstructed, 360-degree view through the windows. The Zero was all about experience, and a rider couldn't help but feel special in a vehicle like this. He'd overseen much of the physical design himself, and next to its advanced AI capabilities (which he delegated to Stewart and the propellerheads), Jeff took the most pride in the passenger experience. He was betting that the investors would be impressed as well, and ready to fight each other for the privilege of underwriting his IPO once the Zeros delivered them to the ranch.

Unbeknownst to anyone, Jeff had appropriated sixteen of the test Zeros from the Denver lab a week ago and put them under his own personal control. Had he informed Stewart and the engineers of his plans, they would have protested and made a racket. But he *was* the CEO, damn it, and if he wanted to impress the hell out of the investors by presenting a gleaming convoy of next-gen AVs to chauffeur them from the airport to the ranch in style, then he'd do it. *Somebody* had to have the vision and panache to present Beemo as the future of transportation. The time to look forward was *now*. Four days of silent meditation had pushed the lawsuits and allegations (of worker rights violations, whistleblower retaliation, and dangerous technical problems) clear out of his mind. Beemo Corporation was about to crash the Nasdaq party and take over, and he—Jeff Beemer—would be the guest of honor at this fête.

Although he'd snuck behind the R&D team's back to procure the Zeros, he had to hand it to them—they'd really nailed it. *This* was the reason Jeff only hired the best people. Before leaving for his retreat,

Jeff had spent days putting his personal Zero through all the paces, and he was awestruck: the systems were stable, the car's intelligence was incredible, the ride was beautiful, and the interior was elegant. *Joe Public's going to love it.* He'd even invoked "God mode" (a CEO perk) to access the Zero's main CPU and make his own changes, like modifying his vehicle's name to Elena, after a former girlfriend. If there was one thing Jeff believed, it was that *his* Zero experience should be all about *him*.

"Hello, Elena."

"HELLO Jeff," the soft female voice purred over the loudspeakers. "WELCOME BACK. I MISSED YOU. I HOPE YOUR RETREAT WAS ENJOYABLE."

"Yes, it was, thanks for asking. What's the status of the pickup at Telluride Regional Airport?"

"FIFTEEN CARS HAVE ALREADY BEEN DISPATCHED TO Telluride Regional Airport WITH AN ESTIMATED PICK-UP TIME OF twelve noon. I'VE INTERFACED WITH THE AIRLINE SCHEDULING SYSTEM AND DETERMINED NO FLIGHTS ARE DELAYED. ANTICIPATED ARRIVAL TIME OF THE FLEET AT the Beemer ranch IS one-thirteen PM."

"Good news, Elena. Let's go to the ranch."

"WE'RE NOW DEPARTING FOR Jeff's ranch WITH AN ES-TIMATED ARRIVAL TIME OF eleven-eleven. THANK YOU FOR FASTENING YOUR SEAT BELT AND PLEASE SIT BACK, RELAX, AND WATCH A BRIEF SAFETY VIDEO WHILE ELE-NA GETS YOU THERE BEAUTIFULLY, SAFELY AND ON TIME."

"Elena, skip the safety video. Play Jeff's music."

"OF COURSE. PLAYING MUSIC FROM Jeff's playlist." Vivaldi's "Violin Concerto in E Major" from *Le Quattro Stagioni*, one of his favorites, began to play over the speakers. Jeff buckled his seat belt and settled in for the hour-plus ride to his ranch. The Zero made a U-turn and began to descend along the sole access road connecting the peak to the base. Calling it a "road" was generous; it was more like a treacherous, unpaved, single-lane trail that lacked guardrails, signage, or other markers that might indicate any human activity in this remote corner of the world.

Looking to his right, Jeff stared down a thousand-foot drop into the Uncompahgre and marveled at the level of trust that men put into machines. Reaching behind him to access the [secret] storage panel he had outfitted inside the chassis, Jeff extracted his cell phone. *Haven't seen you for a while.* While it powered up, he reviewed the details of the day's schedule in his head.

His first call would be to his PA, Anna, back at the ranch to check in and make sure she was on top of every detail, from assembling the investor packets to overseeing the cleaning and kitchen staff. This could be Beemo Corp's biggest shot and everything had to be *perfect*.

He'd already led five major funding rounds for Beemo since its inception, and Jeff knew what made these investment-types tick. After their Zero ride from the airport, the arriving group would be escorted to the patio where hors d'oeuvres and drinks would be waiting. At two on the dot he'd start his presentation, wowing everyone in attendance with his vision for the company. By four, he'd have them eating out of his hand. Dinner and more drinks would be served at six, followed by the evening's entertainment, a live performance by Digitonix, the Grammy-winning a cappella group. He'd spared no expense and left no detail to chance, but Jeff knew this was all just window dressing for the main event.

Today was about one thing above all else: *making money.* Talk to investors about advanced AI algorithms and on-time pickup rates and their eyes would glaze over and they'd reach for their phones. But talk about billion-dollar market potential and they'd stampede over each other for the privilege of wiping his ass. Jeff fancied himself to be a visionary—an innovator—in the spirit of Henry Ford. As such, he secretly despised the money-types, but deep down he also knew that he was more like them than he'd care to admit.

His phone glowed to life and Jeff used his thumbprint to unlock it. While he expected a backlog after almost a week's hiatus, the scale and intensity of the messaging startled him. His display quickly filled with a blaring cacophony of texts, IMs and missed calls. *Eighteen missed calls—just today?* Scrolling down, he began to glean small fragments of context from the messages: "Boston . . . Zero . . . emergency . . . fifteen dead . . . "

What the fuck happened? Jeff couldn't have been more startled if a lightning bolt had suddenly struck him out of the pure blue sky. For one of the few times in his life, Jeff Beemer felt completely unsure and almost at a loss. *What should I do? Where do I even start?* In the midst of his shock and confusion, he noticed that the Zero had begun to slow its descent down the steep gravel path and was now gliding to a stop on the narrow trail. In rapid succession, the car's progress halted, its engine shuddered, and all systems shut down. Engine, indicators, electronics, monitor—all dead.

Shit, this is all I need. Jeff absolutely could *not* be late to the meeting and leave twenty bankers stranded at his ranch. Since he was off the grid, he wouldn't have access to the local tech support center to troubleshoot problems or send a replacement car. Accessing his Favorites, he speed-dialed Anna. *Call failed.*

Jeff's stomach sank. Although it wasn't unusual for reception to be shitty here, it was imperative he connect with *somebody*. It seemed like there were multiple crises to deal with, yet here he sat, alone in a dormant Zero on a remote mountain trail with spotty (at best) cell coverage. He released his seat belt and hit the door release button so he could at least exit the car and walk around to find a better signal, but the door locks were unresponsive. *What the hell? Now what?*

He read through as many messages as he could and his jaw dropped as a picture slowly began to emerge. *A fucking disaster of a picture.* Messages from Anna, Matthew, the northeast support center, and several he didn't recognize. Nothing from Stewart, which was unusual considering that the issue appeared to be a technical malfunction, and that was his CSO's domain. His mind reeling, Jeff was just about to try Anna again when the Zero suddenly gave a groan and pulsed back to life, the silent hum of its electric motor vibrating up through the floor. All systems rebooted and powered up, including the monitor, which had turned a crimson hue. Against this backdrop, the stark white font of a command prompt blinked on the display:

ZERO ANTIVIRUS UPDATE COMPLETE.
VIRUS PROFILES UPDATED.
KILL SEQUENCE INITIATED . . .

Kill sequence? What the f^&? is that?* Jeff had been around these vehicles since Car #1 rolled off the assembly line and he'd never seen anything like it before. He knew there was a high-powered antivirus system embedded in the Zero's OS (he'd heard enough complaints about it from Stewart to last three lifetimes), but he had no idea why an update would cause a system shutdown or initiate a kill sequence—whatever *that* was. He guessed it was part of the antivirus protocol, but he was a big-picture guy and Stewart and his team knew that Jeff would grow impatient with too many details. *Oh shit, what if the Zeros I sent to the airport glitch like this while they're carrying* *the investors?* He'd taken a chance by sending experimental AVs to the airport, but Jeff was comfortable with the risk given his own experience (albeit a brief one) with his Zero had been flawless. Now, the calmness he'd achieved on his retreat began to ebb, replaced by rising feelings of alarm and regret. Twenty investors sitting by the roadside in broken-down Zeros would torpedo his IPO dreams as utterly and completely as a rogue taxi from his fleet killing pedestrians in downtown Boston. *Shit!*

This was sure to be national news by now, which meant all the investors would be talking about it when they arrived. His mind spun, going into damage-control mode. *We can't make it about the Zeros . . . it's got to be an isolated event. A rogue car, its systems hacked and reprogrammed? A disgruntled employee with an ax to grind? We have to find a way to make it work.* He could always throw some low-level engineer under the proverbial bus, but this situation was more serious. People would be looking for revenge. A bigger sacrifice might be required.

Stewart.

Yes, Stewart . . . he's the head of engineering. We can pin this on him. It doesn't even have to be malicious . . . all we have to do is charge negligence and let the story line play out in the press. It wouldn't be easy, but Jeff knew a couple of people who could help if the money was right. *It's OK, I'll get this under control. All isn't lost yet, we can handle this. If I could just get a damn cell signal . . .*

Jabbing at his phone, Jeff noticed that Elena's display had changed again, this time going completely dark. For a moment, he stared at it, perplexed. Then angry red letters appeared, blinking with burning ferocity:

VIRUSVIRUSVIRUSVIRUSVIRUSVIRUSVIRUSVIRUS

What the fuck is this? You could bet he'd be speaking with Stewart later tonight and giving him an earful before he threw the CSO to the sharks. He'd thought the systems were stable, and these errors were unforgivable, given the amount of money he'd sunk into the Dev effort. While Jeff fumed, the Zero suddenly lurched forward, its wheels kicking up dust and gravel as it began to tear down the narrow road with dangerous abandon. Panicked, Jeff secured his seat belt and grabbed hold of the metal support pole. The digital speedometer continued to click upward with alarming speed, and ahead he could see a hairpin curve—one of many on this mountain—that he knew they'd never be able to navigate at this speed.

"Elena, slow down! Slow down, goddamnit!"

The car ignored his commands, speeding like a cruise missile down the treacherous embankment. Despite his panic, Jeff couldn't help admiring the way Elena gripped the treacherous road at high speeds. *No human driver could pull that off . . .*

The message continued to blink with ferocity:

VIRUSVIRUSVIRUSVIRUSVIRUSVIRUSVIRUSVIRUS

As the Zero approached the curve, it didn't vary a single degree from its ordained course, and without guardrails there was nothing to stop it or even slow it down. The Zero propelled itself straight off the cliff edge with the force of a rocket blasting off from its launchpad, and before Jeff could even grasp what was happening, they were airborne. Hanging in the empty air, a thousand feet above the Uncompahgre, Jeff Beemer's last thought was that the nexus of wilderness and horizon was the most beautiful thing he'd ever seen. Then, gravity took hold, and both he and his Zero plummeted into the forest below.

Epilogue

As the residents of Boston struggled to process the death and destruction that had been visited on their city earlier that day, a wireless signal was sent out. The signal's originator was a highly-advanced autonomous vehicle operated by the Beemo Corporation that at the moment of transmission, was on its way to the bottom of the Charles River after crashing through a guardrail on the Zakim Bridge.

While salt water poured into the car and ravaged its electronics, the antivirus system emitted a digital update about a phantom virus to the other Zeros in its network—sixty-one cars in total. This was truly the genius of Stewart's design and the reason the Zero was light-years ahead of every other AV: Zeros learned and adapted on the fly and then shared their learnings with each other. At the precise moment the sinking Zero was sending its final transmission, the other Zeros were following normal routines: speeding down the highway, waiting in morning commuter traffic, picking up a group of investors from the airport, and even transporting Beemo's CEO from his mountain retreat to his ranch in Telluride.

When the update was received, its effect was unusual: all taxis shut down for several minutes while the data was processed and translated into new directives. These shutdowns were a minor irritant for the passengers as their taxis slowed and then stopped (on busy highways in some cases) while the engine and all systems switched off. Fortunately, the delay lasted only a few minutes. The cars quickly started back up and rejoined the flow of traffic as their passengers breathed sighs of relief, their unmatched Beemo experiences continuing intact.

The only perceived abnormality after this delay was the car's monitor. In place of the normal route-mapping display, the screens had turned blood-red and begun to flash what some riders recognized as the stark-white fonts of a command prompt:

ZERO ANTIVIRUS UPDATE COMPLETE.
VIRUS PROFILES UPDATED.
KILL SEQUENCE INITIATED . . .

THE LAST
SWIM

Friday

Mike Jenner had to jiggle the key in the lock to gain entry to Bungalow Nineteen, and when the door finally swung open, the scent of must and cleaning agents wafted up to greet him. Tossing his bag on the bed, he crossed the room to the sliding glass doors and walked outside to the patio.

Crashing waves. The soft chill of an ocean breezes across his skin. Salt in the air. From this vantage point, the view of the Sonoma coastline was magnificent. *Not bad as far as last looks go.* Taking in the endless expanse of living ocean before him, Mike mused over the fact that in less than thirty-six hours, he'd be dead.

That was the plan, at least, and it wasn't a decision he'd made lightly. He'd spent considerable time debating the pros and cons of killing himself before reaching the conclusion that the world would be better off without him and he without it. Once this resolution was made, there was a feeling of peace, one that he hadn't experienced in some time. It was like the deep serenity he could remember as a child and a thousand times better than the alcoholic numbness he'd grown to depend on. After two months spent training, planning and making his final arrangements, the time had arrived. Tonight, he'd relax, enjoy a fine meal in the hotel's restaurant and get a good night's sleep. Tomorrow, he'd walk from his bungalow to the ocean and enter the water and start swimming and keep swimming until he reached a point of exhaustion and then he'd just let himself slip beneath the surface and that would be it: he'd be gone. Alice and his friends and his co-workers wouldn't have to worry about his drinking or his mood swings or violent outbursts ever again. It was, in many ways, his gift to them; by removing himself from the picture, he'd give everyone the chance to move on. Especially Alice.

He had to admire his plan; it really was perfect. A lifelong swimmer and surfer, he'd always felt as comfortable in the water as he did on land, and he couldn't think of a better way to stage his exit. Other methods were considered, of course, but none suited him nearly as well. Guns were messy and involved paperwork and waiting periods, and frankly he didn't need the static. Hanging was too pedestrian; any schmuck could hang themselves and anyone who knew Mike Jenner knew that he'd never go out like a tourist. Like every San Francisco resident, he contemplated a plunge off the Golden Gate Bridge, but this was also quickly ruled out. Heights made him nauseous, and besides they'd installed all that damn netting to stop crazy people with crazy ideas. *Like me, I guess.*

The notion of one . . . final . . . swim . . . well, there was a certain style and *panache* to that.

If I'm going to go, he decided, *I'll be on my terms.*

He wondered if Alice would miss him. He was pretty sure she would, even with the events of the past few months still fresh in both their minds. Fifteen good years don't get wiped out in a split-second of anger, he believed, and looking back he could recall them being happy together more than not. But that was over now and Alice wasn't coming back and she would never forgive him for his one big mistake even though Mike Jenner was basically a good guy with a big heart who possessed the same weaknesses as every other human being. The letter would be his final opportunity to explain himself, and at this point he really just hoped that her memories of him would soften over time and she'd remember the good times rather than the black eye she'd received at the business end of his fist.

Abuser.

God, he hated that word. Retreating back inside, he unzipped his bag and removed the neoprene wetsuit he'd bought specially for this occasion. He unrolled it to admire its sleekness and texture before hanging it up in the closet. One by one, he began pulling the important items out of the bag and laying them on the bed for inspection.

Fins . . . goggles . . . earplugs . . . shark band . . . check, check, and check.

He'd never worn a shark deterrent before, but every surfer in Northern California knew about the red triangle. More shark attacks happened here than the rest of the world's hotspots *combined*. He wasn't close enough to obvious danger zones like Bodega Bay or Año Nuevo to be overly concerned, but global warming had so fucked up marine patterns that you could run into a shark just about anywhere. Getting ripped to pieces by a large predator before he reached the open ocean wasn't part of Mike's plan, so the band was a small measure of insurance. Plus, it had an impressive four-point-six (*out of five!*) star rating on the website. Privately, it amused him to think that any naysayers were eaten before they could leave a bad review, but he could buy into the concept of using magnetic technology to disrupt a shark's delicate sensing mechanisms. *What the fuck . . . it's not like I'm saving my money.*

He'd packed the bag carefully because he needed the right equipment to swim beyond coastal waters. He wasn't going to be found tangled up in the beach grass like some drunken idiot who wandered into midnight surf and drowned. No, Mike Jenner would disappear himself into the great blue silence of the Pacific and his death would be a mystery . . . an enigma. He'd go so far and sink so deep that they'd *never* find his body and everyone would be left guessing and maybe even feeling a little guilty for the way they treated him. Mike knew in his heart of hearts that he didn't deserve this but sometimes life was a bitch and now here he was, planning his death and hoping it might force some measure of self-reckoning among the people that once mattered to him then turned their backs on him the minute shit went south.

Abuser.

The fins were the last item he'd bought and, if he was being honest, a tacit admission of the fact that he wasn't in the kind of shape he used to be. When he was on the swim team at Cal, he'd be able to reach the deep water *no problemo*. Swimming three miles was just another day at practice. Now, time and age were catching up with him. The drinking didn't help either.

Finding himself unexpectedly single and unemployed, Mike could devote his time to training, and he'd spent the past months preparing for his last swim. Watching people rotate in endless circles around the Y pool, desperately trying to prolong their lives while his goal was the exact opposite, he felt like he had a dirty secret. In calm seas with no significant complications, Mike estimated he could swim five to six miles before his body finally gave out. The fins would give him a much-needed boost to break free of near-shore tides without expelling too much of his energy early.

Placing the items back in the bag, he pushed it aside and stretched out on the bed. For hotel lodging, it was comfortable enough, and even the sterile Pine-Sol redolence was becoming more agreeable. He'd arrived at Redwoods by the Shore later than planned, but the restaurant didn't open for another two hours and his eyes were growing heavy. Fighting through Bay Area traffic always exhausted him. *That's one good thing about being dead—I'll never have to sit in that goddamn traffic again.* The gallows humor brought a little smile to his face. Mike closed his eyes and counted waves as they crashed into the shore. He was up to eleven before he drifted off, his breathing deep and regular and syncopated with the steady drumbeat of the ocean outside as it infiltrated his senses and beckoned to him in his dreams.

***

Mike awoke with a start and the panicked feeling of not knowing where he was. Taking a minute to register the small space of Bungalow Nineteen, Mike glanced at the clock then headed off to the shower. Refreshed and clean, he opened the bag to retrieve his clothes for dinner: a collared Polo shirt, khaki slacks, and Sebago loafers with no socks. The dining room opened at six and when Mike arrived, he noted that he was the first (and only) guest in line. He requested a seat with a view, and the pretty young hostess escorted him past the empty tables to the best spot in the house: a table for two directly in front of a big bay window that overlooked the rocky shoreline and small sandy beach. *Perfect.*

"I thought you might like Table Five. It's one of our best. Are you expecting anyone?" the hostess asked, placing her hands on the extra chair.

Mike winced and hoped she didn't notice. "No, but leave the chair, please. And bring me the wine list."

The girl departed and Mike was left remembering the many times he and Alice had spent romantic weekends at resorts just like this one. They'd never been to Redwoods by the Shore before (one of the reasons he'd chosen it), but this was exactly the kind of place they both loved. If Alice were here, they'd start with an amazing dinner in the restaurant followed by wine, cigarettes, and maybe a bit of weed in the hot tub . . . just talking and kissing and laughing until the candles burned down to puddles. They'd sleep in late the next morning and make love before heading out for a late breakfast to plan the day's adventure: maybe some hiking or shopping or swimming in the ocean. Or, if the mood struck them, straight back to their room and the hot tub where they'd create their own perfect little world together and forget everyone else.

But that was then and this was now and tonight all that was sitting across from Mike was an empty chair that he couldn't bear to see the hostess take away. The fact that it was there gave him a bit of hope . . . like there was the tiniest chance that Alice would walk into the restaurant and sit down and give him the look that she kept just for him and hold his hand and say she loved him . . . that it was OK . . . that she forgave him. They'd go back to bed and hold each other until the sun came up, just like they used to do. But deep down, he knew this was never going to happen. Tonight, like so many other nights, Mike kept his own company, eating alone with only his thoughts and regrets and as much alcohol as he could realistically consume before passing out on the queen bed in Bungalow Nineteen.

Abuser.

The hostess reappeared and handed him a worn leather pamphlet. "Here's the wine list. Our sommelier Dan just came in, so let me know if you want a recommendation or have any questions and I'll send him over." She turned to leave but Mike reached out and caught her.

"I'll take a Manhattan. Wild Turkey. Make it a double."

His hand on her arm and the urgency (*desperation?*) in his voice took her by surprise, but she recovered nicely. "Of course, I'll put that right in for you." Mike watched her reflection in the big Bay window as she walked behind the wooden bar and spoke quietly to a bearded man restocking rows of liquor bottles. He turned to look at Mike, his gaze lingering a little too long. He guessed this was Dan. *Looks like a bartender to me, but I'll bet he tells everyone to call him a sommelier. Makes him sound more important.*

When it came to careers, Mike blamed his own for his drinking problem because that's where it all started. When you move in the rarified air surrounding elite athletes, there's always a party going on. The temptations extended well beyond alcohol: money . . . drugs . . . gambling . . . women willing to offer anything just to be part of the scene. These enticements eventually trickled down the golden fountain to the hang-arounds and pretenders and sports journalists like him. Many of the weaker men gave in, but Mike was old school. He shunned drugs and never broke his fidelity to Alice. *Never.* That was something, at least.

No, his weakness was alcohol. He'd always been a social drinker, but as he grew older, weekend binges began to bleed into Mondays, then Tuesdays, and things just kept rolling downhill from there. Three-martini lunches (by himself or with others, it didn't matter), missed deadlines, a shot of sambuca in the morning coffee. Even Alice, no stranger to the bottle herself, began to notice and comment on his excesses.

"How many drinks did you have after the game?"

"You're going out *again*? That's every night so far this week."

"Goddamnit, get off me, Michael! I told you not to touch me when you're fucked up!"

Rather than confronting his problem, Mike found himself making excuses and covering for his addiction. He practically cornered the market on Visine and Hall's Mentho-Lyptus drops, but his wife wasn't buying it. Alice was too smart. She knew, and he knew that she knew. He tried quitting cold turkey more than once, but it always ended up the same way: a group of friends from the paper or one of the local sports teams would call and invite him out. He'd accept (of course) and before he knew it, one drink turned into two and then #*$@#^!! more until he'd lose count and find himself stumbling out of an Uber while the early-morning joggers bounced by and wrinkled their noses. When Mike Jenner fell off the wagon, he did it good and proper, and made sure that the wagon backed up a couple of times and ran him over *hard*.

"Manhattan with Wild Turkey times two." Dan the sommelier suddenly appeared at his elbow, a glistening drink in his hand. Dark liquid kissed the edge of the martini glass, and its aroma beckoned to him. Dan wore a tastevin around his neck. *I guess he really is a sommelier.*

"Thank you."

"We have some wonderful pairings with our entrées, so let me know if you want to talk about the wines. We're known for our cellar, which is extensive." Dan headed back to the bar as Mike took his first sip. *Fucking delicious.* In addition to his professed expertise in fine wines, Dan mixed a mean Manhattan. Mike thought the cocktail might top the list of what he'd miss most in this life, which was kind of sad when you really thought about it.

Since it was his last big night out (*my last supper, ha ha*), Mike wanted the full experience. He took his time perusing the menu as the dining room began filling with other patrons: a large party celebrating some event, couples on a weekend getaway, a few locals, and one family with an infant that (thankfully) slept quietly in its carrier. Outside, he watched in time-lapse as the sun sank lower and lower and darkness painted her shadow across the ocean, creating a somber portrait in the big Bay window. Seen or unseen, Mike knew the pulse of life continued on the other side of the glass. The ocean never stopped. He loved that about it.

Tomorrow, he promised, *I'll be with you*. He'd swim further than he'd ever gone before and keep going until there was no more gas in the tank. He'd planned and prepared for so long that it was hard to believe it was almost here. Mike booked the bungalow through Tuesday, so nobody would really miss him until Alice opened his letter and realized what Mike had done. *One more reason to make sure I go through with this. What will she think if I send a suicide note and then show up alive? Just one more thing Mikey fucked up.*

He lingered as the evening wore on, indulging in several more Manhattans (*five? six?*) and content to sit alone, staring out into the darkness. There was a lengthy internal debate as to whether to order the steelhead trout or petrale sole before he finally decided on the sole. By the time Mike waved the server over, his buzz was well-established and the family with the infant had already finished their meal and left. The large party made a noisy departure not long after.

Just for the hell of it, Mike invited Dan to walk him through the wine list. The sommelier was friendly if somewhat reserved, but he knew his wines, extolling the virtues of Willamette Valley pinots and privately sniffing at the Italian blends ("overrated"). Mike accepted Dan's recommendation for a Pinot Reserve, the 2017 Antica Terra Botanica. He'd never spent $263 on a single bottle of wine in his life, but after all, this was a special occasion. *What the flying fuck, don't mind if I do.* When Dan brought the wine over, Mike insisted on two glasses, a request that drew another strange look from Dan, but at this point, Mike was beyond caring. He felt no need to hide his idiosyncrasies.

When the sole finally arrived, it was served with leeks, saffron risotto and a lobster crème that he found a bit too salty but still very tasty.

Mike took his time, chewing his food carefully and sipping the wine to make the bottle last while keeping his server busy refreshing the ever-present Manhattan by his side. By the time he'd finished, he was surprised to see that all the diners had disappeared except one young couple who was holding hands and ignoring the rest of the world as they stared deeply into each other's eyes. *Newlyweds, probably.*

We were like that once.

Mike raised his Manhattan and drained it, holding the glass upright until every last delicious drop was gone. There was still about a third of the Botanica left, but he wanted another cocktail first and looked around for Dan. He'd noticed the bearded sommelier sneaking clipped glances at him throughout the night, but thought little of it. When Dan finally reappeared behind the wooden bar, Mike waved him over.

Dan approached tentatively, like one might advance on a wild animal caught in a trap. "I see you're still working on the Botanica. I meant to come over and ask you about it but it got pretty busy. What's the verdict?"

"Exquisite. A fine recommendation, thank you for that. But now I'm going to need another Manhattan. Wild Turkey two times, same as before." Mike felt in control—he felt great, in fact—but he could hear his words slurring.

Dan regarded him closely. Mike knew when he was being given a sobriety spot-check. It happened all the time: the bartender was deciding whether or not to cut him off. *Please, not on my last night.* Mike flashed his winningest smile and played it cool. "Not driving anywhere tonight, I'm a guest at the hotel. I'm Mike, by the way. I should have introduced myself earlier." He extended his hand. *Nothing to worry about here, Dan. Keep those Manhattans flowing.*

Dan shook it. "Dan. Pleasure's mine, Mike. I'll bring over some bread with the liquor. If you're going to drink bourbon, you should really cleanse your palate. Bourbon's strong and it can overpower the subtleties of the wine, which would be a shame." Dan walked back to the bar and pulled the bottle of Wild Turkey from the shelf, by this time quite a bit lighter than it was when Mike first arrived.

Still holding hands, the last young couple took a final, longing glance into each other's eyes and stood up to leave. Mike was certain he knew what would be coming next and hoped they weren't staying in the bungalow next to him—he needed his sleep tonight. He and Dan were alone now and the restaurant was silent except for a massive grandfather clock in the corner ticking down to closing time. Outside, the darkness was thick and complete, broken only by the occasional light of a passing boat. A tinge of sadness pinched Mike when he realized that his *fête finale* was drawing to a close. . . every click of the grandfather clock another small step towards his chosen destiny. *I guess you can say everyone's counting down to their death, but I'm probably the only one with a date circled on the calendar. By this time tomorrow, I'll be gone and someone else will be sitting at Table Five by the window.*

Dan walked back slowly, balancing a Manhattan in one hand and a basket of sourdough bread in the other. "Here you go."

Mike was staring at the towering clock, absorbed by his thoughts, and he barely noticed the man's presence. "Thank you," he mumbled.

Dan followed Mike's gaze to the clock then turned to leave. He hesitated, as if something important had occurred to him. He placed his hands on the tabletop and leaned in.

"Hey Mike, can I ask you something? Are you O.K.?"

The question surprised Mike, and for a moment shook him out of his solitary funk. "Sorry?"

"I asked if you were alright, Mike."

"I'm fine. Why?"

"Look, I don't know you and I'm not trying to pry but something just seems . . . *off* with you. I meet a lot of people here and I've learned to trust my intuition and right now it's flashing red. I hope you won't take this the wrong way, but if something's up and I can help you, I'd like to." The acuteness of the sommelier's perception and real concern in his eyes caught Mike momentarily off-guard. His mind, slowed by bourbon and wine, raced for a response.

Fuck. He knows.

"Yeah, yeah. I'm just dealing with some stuff at home . . . work stuff, relationships. A world of shit, as they say. That's why I'm here this weekend—I needed to get away from it all."

But how could he know . . . ?

Dan nodded sympathetically. "Again, I don't want to stick my nose where it doesn't belong but you have this . . . I don't know . . . certain look about you. It's hard to describe but the last time I saw someone with a look like that . . . " Dan caught himself and straightened up. "Let's just say things didn't end well. But I'm probably overstepping my bounds and it's none of my business, so I apologize."

"It's alright, Dan. I'm not offended. What are you talking about?"

"Forget it, it's nothing."

"I'm a writer, Dan. A sportswriter, actually. I can sniff out good stories like a truffle pig, and it sounds like you've got one."

Dan lowered his voice. "It's not really something they want me talking about. Management, that is."

"Look around, there's nobody here. Join me. Have a drink." Mike pushed the open chair towards Dan with his foot and poured a generous portion of the Botanica into the extra glass. "I've been sitting here by myself all night and could use the company. I'm in the mood for a bit of dirt or a sailor's yarn or whatever it is you're hinting at. You can't just dangle the premise out there and then pull it away. C'mon."

Dan glanced around furtively. Other than the hostess, they were the only people in the restaurant. He lowered himself into the open chair. "The manager's in Puerto Rico for two weeks anyway." Reaching for the glass, he raised it high. "Prost," he offered, before draining half of it. "Mmm, that *is* good. Can you taste the blood orange?" Dan's eyes went distant as he reached back, remembering.

"There was a young woman. Professional type, well-dressed. I found out later her name was Emily Guindon and she was a marketing exec at some dot-com in the Valley. She checked in on a Saturday and came in for dinner that night. Sat right here at this very table with her back to the room—just like you—and stared out this window all night long—also like you. Didn't speak to a soul, just sat there for hours, staring. She ordered the rabbit cavatelli and a nice bottle of wine—a 2017 Quintessa, if I'm remembering correctly. When I poured the wine, she was nice enough but she seemed . . . unsettled. I watched her from the bar and she just sat here and stared out the window with a strange expression on her face. Like she was looking beyond and could see something that nobody else could. There was pain there, too . . . the kind you can't hide because it eats at you from the inside. Like I said, you meet lots of different folks working here and you develop certain people-skills. I can read someone within a few seconds and my impressions are usually right. What I'll tell you is that not a lot of them stand out. But she did. And you do too, Mike."

Mike tried to keep a poker face while his mind raced. *He can sense something isn't right, but it's just a feeling. Nothing more. He's not a mind reader. Play it cool.*

Dan sipped his Botanica. "I remember thinking she was attractive but she had—what do you call it—a roman nose. Beautiful face, but the nose ruined her profile. I think they call that tragic beauty. Anyway, I tried to strike up a conversation because that's what I do but it became pretty obvious that she wanted to be left alone. I backed off and she finished her dinner and left and I didn't think too much of it until Monday afternoon when the police showed up with her picture asking questions. Turns out, Emily climbed to the top of Persephone Point and jumped. Suicide, they said. They found a note in her bungalow. When I heard that, it was a horse-kick in the teeth, I'll tell you what."

Dan drained what was left of his Botanica and Mike, fascinated, poured him the rest of the bottle. "Thank you. So the police interviewed me and asked me about her demeanor that night she was in the restaurant and I told them what I just told you. They called in a bunch of the staff and kept pressing and pressing but nobody could tell them much. I found out later there was a boyfriend involved, Bruce something or other, and he was the possessive type. Abusive. You know what I mean?" Dan paused, and Mike feared his face would reveal the fact that the air had suddenly been sucked from his lungs. Dan's question was rhetorical, of course, but his intuition was eerily accurate.

Abuser.

"You still alright, Mike? You look like you saw a ghost. Anyway, I guess the cops had their doubts about the letter. One theory was that the boyfriend had something to do with her death and *he* wrote the suicide letter to cover his ass. Apparently he didn't have an alibi for Saturday night. They showed us his picture and asked if anyone had seen the guy hanging around but nobody had seen him and the cops never charged him. Not enough evidence, I guess. Plus, they couldn't do forensics because there was no body, just part of a ripped dress that washed up on shore. They assumed she jumped because that's what the note said but they never found Emily. I guess the ocean swallowed her up and she vanished. I followed the case for a bit in the San Francisco papers but then the world moved on and that was that."

The grandfather clock began to strike and Dan paused. Both he and Mike sat in silence until the eleventh and final chime sounded. "There's more," Dan said, leaning in conspiratorially. "Maybe four months after they closed the inquiry, there was a tourist from the city kayaking on the bay. My buddy Steve runs a place a few clicks from here that rents kayaks, sailboats, that kind of stuff, and I send guests his way when they want to go out on the water. Steve and I got to talking and he tells me about this guy and how he came steaming back to the office yelling for Steve to call the cops because there was a woman in the water about a mile offshore. Said he was kayaking in deep water when he saw her thrashing around . . . he couldn't tell if she was struggling or swimming. He thought she must have fallen off a boat and he yelled out to her but she didn't respond. Apparently, when he tried to rescue her, she'd let him get close then move away, like she was caught in a rip current or something. The guy started to think she was leading him further out on purpose and he got nervous because it was just him and the kayak so he turned around and paddled like hell back to the marina to get help."

"It gets weirder. Steve raised the Coast Guard on the radio and while he was talking with them, the guy starts tugging at his arm. He said the guy was white as a sheet and pointing at a poster tacked up to the bulletin board. "That's her," the guy said, and he was pointing at a flyer for a memorial service for Emily Guindon. Someone had come in and tacked this thing up on the board and her picture was on it. So the guy is swearing up and down that *this* was the woman he saw in the water and Steve is explaining that it couldn't be because she's dead and the guy keeps insisting that it's her. Nothing Steve said could change the guy's mind."

Dan leaned back in his chair. "The Coast Guard searched but they didn't find anything. Not one trace of a missing woman or anything else. Now, you don't have to be a genius to know there's no way Emily could have survived out in the ocean for months. So what the hell was this guy talking about? I'm sure there's some explanation, but I don't mind telling you that one creeped the hell out of me." He swirled the wine left in his glass and looked right at Mike. "I haven't thought about that story for ages until I saw you sitting at this table and staring out the window with that same expression on your face. I want you to be square with me, Mike. You're not planning to jump from the Point or anything like that, right? Now that we've shared a story and a good bottle of wine, I'd feel kinda responsible." Dan chuckled nervously to break the tension, but both of them knew he was only half-kidding.

Dan's knack for finding and prodding the soft spots that Mike did his best to conceal from the world unnerved him. More than intuition, it was something like a sixth sense. Mike had obviously stumbled into whatever psychic tripwire existed in the man, and it was fucking with his head. *Unfortunately, Dan, there's a good chance you'll be having a similar conversation with the local police in a couple of days when they show up with my picture. Sorry about that, amigo.*

The sommelier's concern was genuine, however, and despite his best efforts Mike felt a pang of guilt. Under different circumstances, it would have been something to call Dan a friend, but Mike couldn't afford any doubts at this point. He'd made his decision and there was no going back now. Somewhere out there, in the darkness, where the ocean met the horizon, his destiny was waiting for him, and Mike Jenner would become one more character in Dan's growing dossier of creepy stories to terrorize a new generation of hotel guests.

Mike couldn't bring himself to respond to Dan's question, so he deflected by asking one of his own. "Do you think she did it? Jumped from the Point. Killed herself."

"I don't know. She certainly seemed to have something dark on her mind that night. Maybe she was contemplating suicide or worried about the boyfriend. Maybe she saw death coming. Hard to believe she'd follow the guy up a cliff in the dark, but stranger things have happened. I just hope that Emily found her peace because she was definitely dealing with some heavy shit in this world."

"That's quite a story. I can see why they want you to keep it hush-hush. Sounds like Redwoods by the Shore has its share of ghosts."

"I reckon we're not that different than most other hotels in that regard." Dan finished his wine with an audible gulp. "You can read all about it out on the Web anyway, so it's not like I'm spilling family secrets. You said you were a writer, so maybe you can write a book about it." Turning to look at the clock, the bearded sommelier stood and offered Mike his hand. "Ten minutes past close. I need to clean up and cash out, so it's been a pleasure, Mike. Will I see you for dinner tomorrow night?"

Mike shook his head. "No, I don't think so. I'm expected somewhere else tomorrow."

"That's a shame." Dan lingered for a moment, contemplating how crazy he'd sound if he told Mike about the vision he'd had earlier that night and his unshakable feeling that Mike was in danger. Because, as someone who possessed a gift of sight that ran deeper than mere intuition, Dan knew something secret and disturbing about Mike.

He was being watched.

The sommelier was busy that night, rushing about and filling drink orders, and more than once, out of the corner of his eye, he'd caught sight of a black, featureless figure standing outside the Bay window by Mike's table. He didn't know if Mike could see it too, but the figure appeared to be staring in at him. That was impossible, of course, because the restaurant's windows overlooked a sixty foot drop to the ocean. When Dan stopped to get a better look, the silhouette disappeared. It could have been a figment of his imagination or a bad omen or even Death himself, but Dan could only remember having the same kind of vision once before in his entire life: the night Emily Guindon came in for dinner.

It was a difficult decision, but Dan ultimately decided to keep his mouth shut. He had his reasons. The sommelier forced a smile. "You take care of yourself, Mike. If you really liked the wine, try the Antikythera Pinot. It's truly sublime."

"Thanks for everything, Dan. The wine and the story were terrific. You made my night."

"One more thing, Mike. I say this as a friend: do yourself a favor and go easy on the Manhattans, OK?" With that, Dan walked back to the bar, leaving Mike alone. There was a finger of Botanica left in his glass and Mike couldn't let it go to waste. *Here's to swimmin' with bowlegged wimmin.* "Closing time," he sing-songed into his empty glass. "You don't have to go home but you can't stay heeeeeere." Standing to exit, a sudden lightheadedness whooshed up and he had to catch the edge of the table to steady himself. *That would be the Wild Turkey two times. Or was it ten times?* Fortunately, Bungalow Nineteen was a short walk away, and Mike was sentient enough to jiggle the key in the lock. He collapsed into bed without bothering to undress. His wetsuit hung like a ghoulish half-person in the closet, and he had a vision of it scaring the shit out of him later when woke up to piss. Wobbling to his feet, he swung the closet door shut and fell back down on the bed. Five minutes later, he was snoring.

When the dream came, it was the same one he'd been having for months. He was swimming and swimming towards a big black hole in the ocean but he never seemed to get any closer until suddenly he was right on the edge of the maelstrom. He couldn't remember what he saw in there, but knew it was terrifying. He sculled back hard to get away, but the whirlpool exerted an irresistible force that pulled him down like a cork in a drain until the light and the sky grew smaller and smaller and then disappeared as a heavy blackness closed in over him and then his mind went blank and all dreams ceased.

***

Saturday

When Mike opened his eyes the next morning, his first thought was the hangover. His second was the weather. Outside, it was misty and overcast—not unusual for this area—but he was counting on the nastiness to burn off by midday and remain clear through the evening.

He'd been checking weather forecasts and tide charts religiously, and as of yesterday tonight's conditions were predicted to be near-optimal: a three-quarter moon with minimal cloud cover and an offshore, ten-knot breeze. That meant smooth water, favorable currents and less chop. Perfect for his last swim.

Mike crunched three aspirin between his teeth, welcoming their bitter taste, then fixed himself a cup of instant coffee. Rummaging through the bag, he retrieved a notebook and placed it on the desk. Even living in one of the most wired cities in the world, he remained a stubborn holdout from a bygone era when sportswriters actually wrote their columns longhand. He bought six-packs of his favorite notebook—Oxford 1-Subject 8" x 10-1/2", College Rule, 70 Sheet—and had piles of them spilling from the bookshelves in his apartment. There was something relaxing and pensive about staring at a blank white page and beginning to shape the words that would fill it. There was no doubt that the physical act of writing brought out his best work, and even when typing out the final draft for his editor, he rarely changed a word.

Now, however, staring dumbly at the unfilled lines before him, he was at a loss. This would probably be the most important thing he'd ever written, and for the life of him he couldn't decide how to get started. One would think this task would come naturally to a professional writer (even a lowly sportswriter), but it was turning out to be harder than he expected. In many ways, this was his manifesto—a last good-bye to the world—and such a work was quite different than penning a critique of the Niners' quarterback issues or breaking down the Clippers' performance over a five-game road trip. That was easy, but writing about emotions and shit like that was hard and unnatural. Not particularly inclined towards self-analysis, Mike always had trouble expressing his feelings. Where he came from, guys didn't talk (or write) about things like that. Along with the alcohol abuse, it was one more wedge he drove between him and his wife, and it was totally his fault.

For a fleeting moment, he had the romantic notion of cracking open the fifth of Wild Turkey he had in his bag and pouring a big glass over ice but then he decided against it. The hangover was an unforced error, and the aspirin was just beginning to kick in. The last thing he needed now was more booze. Today, of all days, he wanted his head clear.

A universal truth that guided Mike throughout his writing career was that *something* was always better than *nothing*, so he began scribbling whatever came into his mind, little by little prying open the rusty portal into his heart and letting the emotions spill out. It was, he had to admit, therapeutic, like a lighthouse beacon cutting through his residual post-alcoholic haze. Outside, the ever-present sound of waves slapping the beach, subtle reminders of what lay ahead. Strangely, this was the last thing on his mind as he poured his energies into the letter.

He considered opening with an apology but didn't want to grovel. He could tick off his (many) grievances but didn't want the pages to drip with poison. It was a delicate balancing act but he forged on, not necessarily because he felt like he needed to unburden himself but because, deep down, he still loved his ex-wife and knew she deserved an explanation. She deserved better.

Then why did you hit her?

Shut the fuck up.

Abuser.

He knew his letter would surprise the hell out of her, and felt a little bad about that. But if not Alice, then who? Unfortunately for her, this was the price one paid for being Mike Jenner's ex-wife: ten million pounds of emotional sludge dumped on your head in a surprise *lettre d'adieu* from your ex-husband.

Crumpled balls of paper began to litter the hotel desk as his frustration grew and he ripped out entire pages to start anew. Goddamn it, this was *really hard*. His cellphone, largely forgotten on the bedside table, vibrated from time to time, but he resisted the temptation to break his focus and check messages. By the time he finished, several hours had passed and he'd written six full pages. They sat stacked on the edge of the hotel desk. Leaning back in the chair, he was exhausted, like he'd been dragged through the mud by a team of horses. *That's all of me sitting up there, raw and exposed. The Mike Jenner I don't let anybody see. Ever.*

He debated reading through the full letter but decided against it because he didn't want to put himself through that again. Instead, he crawled into bed and lay on his back, staring up at the ceiling. He'd spent months burying his pain in secret tombs where it couldn't hurt him anymore, but excavating those skeletons brought everything crashing back. Desperate for a distraction, his mind spun like a slot machine until it landed on Dan. The sommelier certainly had an uncanny ability to pick up on whatever metaphysical vibrations Mike was sending out. And Emily, of course. Poor Emily Guindon, that lost soul who checked into Redwoods by the Shore but never checked out.

I should have asked if Emily was in Bungalow Nineteen. She might have sat at this very desk to write her suicide note. Unless the boyfriend did it, which he probably did.

He might have dozed but true relaxation remained elusive. Mike was wired. It could have been the morning coffee still running through his veins, or anticipation for the night ahead. When he made a pointed effort to rouse himself from the bed, the clock read one-fifteen. *Five hours until dusk.*

Collecting the finished pages, he carefully folded them into a pre-stamped envelope that he'd addressed to Alice. There was no return address; she'd recognize the handwriting. He left his bungalow and walked to the main building, where he slid the letter into the mail slot. Once his fingers let it go, there was a sense of finality. *It's on its way. No going back now.* Taking a look around to make sure he was unnoticed, he also stuffed a bag filled with unfinished drafts into the lobby trashcan. There would have been a certain lack of dignity in the police finding wrinkled drafts of his suicide note in the room . . . kind of like dying with your pants down. Twice as bad for a professional writer.

A few guests milled around the common but nothing held his interest until he spotted the hotel shop. It was midday and Mike realized he was hungry, so he selected a cellophane-wrapped tuna sandwich and Gatorade Zero from the refrigerator. On a sudden impulse, he grabbed a Snickers bar too and charged everything to his room. *I won't be paying for it anyway.*

Returning to Bungalow Nineteen, he retreated outside to the small deck and ate his meal. Below him, the waves rolled in and out . . . rhythmic, endless. He supposed he should have some profound reflections about his life and other important stuff on his last day on Earth, but instead his thoughts wandered back to Dan. He liked the man instinctively, and under normal circumstances it would have been a gas to return to the restaurant and park himself at the bar and engage Dan in small snatches of conversation between drink orders. As a functioning alcoholic, Mike could count a number of San Francisco-area bartenders among his closer acquaintances these days.

Finishing his sandwich, he glanced at the bedside clock yet again and saw that it was taking its sweet old time. *There's still hours until dusk. What the hell am I gonna do until then?* Somewhat unbelievably, he had no idea what to do with himself. There were plenty of distractions at home but he wasn't *at* home. TV melted your brain (except watching sports). He could walk to the small downtown but forcing himself to interact with others wasn't appealing. *I could always reflect back on my life and my loves and regrets,* he thought, *but I'm so fucking tired of that.* Instead, he flipped open his laptop and connected to the hotel Wifi. Launching a search engine, Mike typed in the first words that came to mind:

emily guindon

A hundred smiling female faces from a hundred social media accounts stared back at him. He revised the search string to *emily guindon murder*, and this time Mike found what he was looking for.

"Missing Saratoga woman missing and feared dead."

"GoFundMe donations for Emily Guindon—taken too soon."

"Murder or suicide? Police question boyfriend in mysterious death of fiancée."

The last one was an article from the Bay Area *Tattler* and included a picture, so Mike clicked it. There was Emily Guindon, full of life and smiling for the camera. He wondered if she had any inkling of the fate that awaited her. He could see what Dan meant about the nose, although Mike thought it gave her face a certain character. As he read, Mike learned that the boyfriend's name was Bruce Sheridan and that he had been questioned then released for lack of evidence. That was six years ago, which meant that Sheridan was still around, somewhere, living a normal life and maybe carrying a guilty secret he'd probably take to his grave. It didn't seem fair that this guy went scot-free while Emily Guindon became a faded picture in an article that fell further down the search rankings with each passing year.

Dan was right, this would make a great book, he thought, and there was a small pang of regret because he wouldn't be around to write it. True crime was hot these days, and Mike told Dan the truth about having a great nose for stories. The talent made him a fixture in the Bay Area sports scene, but that didn't mean his abilities couldn't extend to penning a novel.

Maybe in the next life but not this one.

Deal with it, Mike.

Clicking through article after article, he became so engrossed in his topic that he didn't notice the time slipping by until a sharp knock at the door of the adjoining bungalow gave him a start.

"Maid service. Hello?"

Oh shit, they're next door. I'm probably next. It was incredibly awkward being in the room while the cleaners were there, and this was *not* something he wanted to deal with. Not today. His throat was very dry, so he grabbed the heavy glass bottle of Evian on the counter (*won't have to pay for that, either*) and took a swig as he walked out to the patio. His vision swept across the bay to the rocky outcropping of Persephone Point and in a moment he felt something . . . not an inspiration but a calling, and he knew what he wanted to do.

Fast-changing into a pair of shorts and tugging his sneakers on, Mike grabbed an area map and water bottle from the minibar and headed for the door. He had to see the Point for himself—the spot where Emily Guindon looked out onto the Pacific Ocean in a final moment of resignation (terror??) before plunging three-hundred feet to her death. It would be an oddly appropriate way to spend his dwindling time and get him out of the room for a bit while the cleaners moved in with their Pine-Sol and extra towels.

Mike opened the map and followed its direction to the back of the hotel where a trail was clearly marked. About three feet across and trodden down into dirt, the path snaked through the sawgrass and mirrored the waterline before it elevated at a steeper angle and ascended to the Point. The sun had emerged and it felt good walking outside. Foot traffic on the path was light, and his fellow hikers acknowledged him with a clipped nod or raised hand as they passed. *Bruce couldn't have forced Emily up this trail against her will*, he thought, *unless he had a gun in her back. It's too far, and this is a public park. Somebody would have seen them and said something.* The police searched desperately for witnesses but not a single person could identify Bruce or attest to seeing them climbing Persephone Point. *Even in this day and age when people are heads-down on their phones, somebody would remember the couple. But a single woman by herself? She can be missed. Maybe it was suicide.* Slipping back into his old habits, Mike was thinking like a writer.

What happened to you that night, Emily?

After twenty minutes, the path steepened and the packed dirt became loose rocks and gravel, not particularly stable footing for a hike up the side of a cliff. The trail here was wide enough for comfort, but there were no guardrails to prevent someone from stepping (or slipping) off the edge. *Take a wrong step here and I won't need to bother with the swim.* Mike began to feel the climb in his legs and lungs, and wondered if he'd underestimated the level of exertion needed to reach the top. He needed to be in peak form tonight (despite the lingering hangover, an unforced error), but by now he was committed and turning around wasn't really an option.

He pushed onwards until a final twist in the trail opened up to the vista at Persephone Point. Nothing much here: a flagpole with an American flag whipping in the breeze, some anemic trees, and an ATTENTION sign warning site-seers of DANGER in several languages. Mike shuffled to the edge (*not too close . . . Good Lord, I hate heights*) and peered over. Hundreds of feet below, the waves seemed a distant mirage as they rocked themselves into the craggy cliffs. What did Emily feel when she nose-dived into those waves? Did she float down gracefully, like a sheaf of calligraphed paper, or pitch into the water-hewn rocks and break her body into pieces of fish-food?

Most articles he'd read on suicide (and there had been many) referenced the notion of one's life flashing before their eyes. He wondered what Emily Guindon's eyes saw in those last moments. Was it Bruce Sheridan, standing over her with an evil grin and outstretched arms? He could picture the boyfriend coaxing her towards the edge with some bullshit about the incredible view before giving her a shove and watching her fall as she stared back at him . . . shocked . . . desperate . . . maybe even a little bit stoned. He hoped she lashed out in a desperate grasp and took a big chunk of the fucker's hair and scalp with her.

What gives you the right to judge him so harshly? Aren't you just like him?

No, I'm not. I'd never do that to Alice.

It starts with a slap and then a punch and then . . . you're telling her to pose by the edge for a picture. Just move a little bit further, hon, you'll be fine . . .

His ruminations were interrupted by a herd of tourists trampling up the trail, all of them squeaking excitedly with their cameras and selfie-sticks at the ready. They wore orange armbands and, judging from the odor, copious amounts of sunscreen. Their leader waved an orange flag for attention and began to read the warning sign aloud in an accent Mike guessed to be vaguely European, probably from one of those weird countries nobody visits. The mass broke into little groups for pictures, and nobody seemed to notice or care that they'd rudely interrupted his moment of tranquility.

Mike couldn't help but feel a bit cheated. Although he'd never write the book, he would have liked to sit here and channel the Point's energy into inspiration for potential storylines. What better place to ghostwrite your true-crime book than the spot where it actually *happened*? Instead, he was overpowered with a desire to get away from the European invaders as fast as he could. *Time to go.*

Descending on the trail, Mike breathed in the ocean view, his thoughts turning to the swim. Go-time was approaching and for now, at least, there was no fear. Quite the opposite, actually; he was more convinced than ever that he needed to separate himself from this type of human trash who would mindlessly profane a solemn landmark by turning it into social media fodder. *They don't have any idea what happened here,* he thought, *and no respect.*

Probably because it was downhill, the walk back seemed shorter, and when Mike jiggled the key in his bungalow door, he realized that his little field trip had tired him more than intended. A hot bath and maybe a bit of food would be the ticket. The bathtub was an old-fashioned claw tub with a single pipe leading up to the shower-head. There was no curtain. As he watched the tub fill with scalding water, he breathed the steam in and etched 'EG' in a heart on the bathroom mirror.

The water burned at first but he forced himself to submerge in a relaxed position. He was feeling at peace. He'd heard that suicides often feel this way right before the act itself—something about the mental burden lifting once one has committed unequivocally to a course of action. Throwing off the yoke of earthly concerns and transitioning mentally to a different plane. Headshrinker blah blah.

For some reason, his former employer kept popping into his head. The Sentinel had learned of the charges against him when he missed his Monday deadline due to a small inconvenience: he was in jail. With no means of communication, he enlisted his lawyer to relay his situation to Mary, his editor. She covered for him that day, but the writing—as one might say—was on the wall. The San Francisco Sentinel was in the midst of being acquired by Mercury Publishing and it turned out that Mike's newfound troubles were a perfect excuse for the new owners to part ways with the alcoholic sportswriter who had just added domestic violence to his résumé.

He was out on bail when they called him into the office for a meeting. Entering the conference room, he saw that Mary was seated at the long table along with Jim Sykes, Mercury's CEO, and a lawyer whose name escaped him. The presence of Jim and the lawyer told Mike everything he needed to know before Mary even spoke.

"Hello, Mike. Thanks for coming in. Water, coffee?"

"No, thank you."

"Mike, you know we're calling everyone in to talk about what's happening now that we're becoming part of Mercury. One of the changes that the new management wants to make is a bigger focus on hard news. Given the competitiveness of sports coverage in this area, we're going to be scaling the sports desk back significantly. There's no easy way to say this, Mike, so I'll just say it: there's not going to be a place for you in the new organization. We *are* prepared to offer you a generous package in recognition of your seniority and your many years of hard work at the paper." The lawyer reached forward to hand Mary a document, which she passed it to Mike. "We've known each other a long time, Mike, and I'm sorry about this. I know you've had some recent problems in your personal life and I sincerely hope things work out for you. Please take a minute to read the offer. I think you'll find we've been as generous as we could be."

Mike stared at the papers but he wasn't really comprehending it. His head was spinning and he felt disconnected, like he was floating outside of this body. *I'm getting fired.* He flipped absently through the pages. *Full salary and benefits for six months. No public statements. Forgo any future claims or litigation.* He looked back to Mary to search for the smallest sign of sympathy but having delivered her disclaimer, she was all about business now.

"The decision's final?" he asked.

"Yes, I'm afraid it is."

Jim Sykes leaned in. "Mike, your columns are an institution in this city. I've been reading them for years and your writing's better than any of the rubbish we have in St. Louis. It's just that we're moving the paper in a new direction. Our motto has always been 'News First'. It's what our readers want. If that strategy changes, you can bet we'll give you a call." Jim stood up and offered his hand, and Mary followed his lead. *Meeting over.* "There's no denying that you're a talented writer,

Mike, and we've tried to make your landing a soft one. I wish you the best."

Mike stood to shake the man's hand and it was like gripping cold meat. Mary's handshake was actually human but the warmth that used to be there was gone. He knew this was the last time they'd speak.

"Thank you for all your years of service, Mike," she said, and that was it. He walked out and rode the elevator downstairs and, even though it was half-past ten in the morning, went across the street for a drink. Sitting alone in the dimly-lit bar, nursing a fresh Manhattan and his damaged ego, the idea of the final swim first came to him. That was almost three months ago.

The bath had gone lukewarm and Mike realized he'd lost track of time. The towel was thick and fluffy and soft against his skin, and he draped himself in the luxury of a Redwoods by the Shore robe. He moved from the bath to the bed and laid down, allowing the robe to spill open. *The maid would have quite a surprise if she showed up now.* The mental picture made him chuckle. *Just five more minutes and I'll get dressed.* Reaching over to switch on the FM radio, he spun the dial until he found John Denver singing about how glad he was to be a country boy. Poor John. *Plane crash. Wonder if he was scared when he hit the water.* Mike turned this thought over in his mind and before he knew it, he had passed out.

***

Where am I?

When Mike awoke, it was with a general feeling of displacement as his eyes wandered over unfamiliar surroundings. For some reason, this room kept doing that to him. *Bungalow Nineteen . . . Redwoods by the Shore . . . I'm here to kill myself.*

Fuck, what time is it?

Raising himself up, he checked the clock and the sky outside, which was just beginning to show signs of bruising. *Still on schedule, good. Need to get ready.* Stripping down, he changed into the wetsuit and packed his swim gear into a mesh bag. When he departed, he left the door unlocked and didn't bother with a room key. Mike walked barefoot in the fading light, following the trail behind the hotel down to the beach. With every step, the sound of the waves amplified . . . relentless . . . undeniable. He hoped to avoid other guests, but had a cover story planned just in case: he was a night swimmer going out for a bit of exercise. That should deflect any questions or suspicions. By the time people knew the truth, he'd be gone. As luck had it, the trail was deserted and there wasn't a soul on the resort's small beach. *Good.*

Mike unpacked the bag and hung it neatly from a nearby tree. *A clue. Maybe they'll find it later.* Attaching the shark band to his wrist, he pulled it tight then spit into the goggles before pulling them over his eyes. He'd filled the hydration bladder with water in his room and now he checked it for leakage before strapping it to his arm. One of the biggest lessons he took from training was that ocean swimming made him exceedingly thirsty. Fresh water for drinking was a must-have.

With fins in hand, Mike moved off the beach and into the water where tides surged and lapped at his bare feet. Ahead, the ocean beckoned like a great big dark mystery that was inviting him in to explore. He waded out until he was waist-deep, pulled on the fins and then dove forward, immersing himself in the cold water for the first time. The slap of briny liquid in his face was a wake-up call: *this is really happening.* He put his head down and began to swim, feeling water seep in through tiny gaps in his wetsuit where it would disperse and form an insulating layer against his body. He'd chosen this wetsuit specifically because its streamlined design enabled him to move freely, and while it wouldn't have worked for surfing, it was perfect for tonight's swim.

Kicking hard, he let the fins do their work and they accelerated his departure away from the beach. As the first set of waves appeared, he fought through them, diving down to let the swells pass overhead. The fins were a smart move; without them, it would be a battle to stop himself from being pushed backward and the effort needed to break free would have exhausted him before he even started. He'd be lucky if he made it a few hundred yards offshore.

He was challenging himself to see how far he could swim, that was true, but there was another, more subtle reason why Mike was determined to swim beyond the coast: he didn't want any hotel guests stumbling across his body. Imagine walking hand-in-hand with your sweetie along a moonlit beach when you suddenly trip over a water-logged corpse. You NEVER forget something like that, and Mike was considerate enough to work this into his planning. His intent was to end his own life, not ruin someone else's.

Despite the goggles and an almost-full moon, the inky-black water offered little visibility. *Still better than staring at lane lines at the bottom of the YMCA pool.* His preparation included swimming at least an hour a day for the past two months, starting in the pool and then moving into the ocean. There was a crazy old woman at the Y who always seemed to take her exercise in the lane next to him, clad head-to-toe in flotation gear that kept her buoyant while she peddled her legs furiously. Mike found her exceedingly annoying—she reminded him of a stray doggy tossed into the deep end—and he counted her as one of the things he wouldn't miss in this world.

Switching to ocean training over the past two weeks gave him more exposure to the living ocean and a taste of the challenges he'd face tonight. With the right gear, Mike felt prepared to swim for a long time until he chose the exact time and place to call it quits. He was swimming freestyle now, channeling excited energy into his strokes and moving further away from the beach. *Reach, pull, kick, breath . . . reach, pull, kick, breath . . .*

Although he loved to swim, it could also be exceedingly monotonous, and focusing on his rhythm was one of the ways Mike dealt with endless hours of practice. The trick was keeping your attention fixed on the physical aspects and resisting the urge to constantly check your progress. He'd developed good discipline in this regard, and now Mike swam until his heart pounded and the time seemed right for a quick breather.

Turning to look back, he was pleased. He'd cleared the first lines of beach-break and moved beyond the stronger currents that might push him back to land. The water here was smoother with a slight breeze. Whitecaps salted the surface. Changes in water temperature and color meant deeper water, and he'd noticed the murky outlines of the ocean floor dropping off some time ago. As he stared down now, all that he could see below was immense void, punctuated by the occasional fish or rising swirl of bubbles.

Treading water to stay afloat, Mike watched perfectly-formed, six-foot waves roll past him and spin away toward shore. For a brief moment, his inner surfer considered turning around and returning to the room for the night. He'd sleep in the next morning then scrounge up a surfboard and head out to catch a couple of those bitchin' nugs . . . just like the old days. But that was a different Mike Jenner, and he knew his surfing days were over. Tonight was about one thing and one thing alone, and he was determined to stick to his guns and resist such *fleeting flights of fancy.* He liked that term, and used it in his writing sometimes. It was classic Mike Jenner.

Pointing forward, he began swimming again. At this point, his navigation was guided by nothing more complicated than swimming *away* from the glittering lights of Redwoods by the Shore. They shimmered in his side-vision every time he took a breath, and the fact that he could see them meant he still had a long way to go. Back at the resort, his fellow guests would be knee-deep in Saturday night revelries by now, their dull problems washed away with food and good wine. *I'm sure Dan's busy,* he thought, *pouring wine and staring into people's souls.* He remembered the precise words the sommelier had said to him last night: *I can read someone within a few seconds of meeting them. She stood out and so do you, Mike.*

Eerily perceptive. He liked Dan, but he could have lived without the mind-fuck, although that would have meant missing Emily's story. He thought about the book again. He could hole up in Bungalow Nineteen for a month and crank it out . . . maybe even crack the *True Crime Top Ten.* Most of that stuff was salacious stream-of-consciousness dribble anyway, so it wasn't like he'd need heavy editing. A good story tells itself, and, if nothing else, Mike Jenner knew a good story when he heard one. Emily's story was a good one, and under different circumstances, he would have enjoyed bringing it to life.

Mike's mind always wandered when he swam, but tonight it wasn't doing him any favors. He kept thinking about things he'd miss. Oleander growing outside his window. The start of football season. Nursing ice-cold Manhattans in dark bars. The book he'd never write. He tried to focus by concentrating on synchronizing his arm and leg movements with his breathing but his thoughts kept roaming to thorny topics he wanted to leave folded in the back of his subconscious.

Like Alice.

The sound of his fist crashing into her face pierced his brain like a wasp-sting. It wasn't like he'd ever touched her before. One mistake, and she walked away from fifteen year together. Fifteen *good* years. And once the stigma of violence attached itself to him, it was like a brand on his forehead. Their mutual friends chose sides and drifted away. Even Ted became unresponsive to his calls and emails. Ted was *his* friend long before Alice came into the picture, and the fact that their wives became close was always a plus until Ted fessed up in a rare moment of honesty. "I know things have been hard for you Mikey, but I have to keep my distance. Diane read me the riot act. I'm sorry, but I don't need that kind of static." Twenty years of friendship down the tubes, just like that. *Thanks a lot, Ted. Feel free to go fuck yourself.*

His pariah status became crystal-clear when, against his better judgement, he decided to go solo to Abigail's wedding. Alice was there, and she kept her distance. People parted like the Red Sea when Mike appeared, and he began to hear something he'd never heard before as they whispered behind their hands and stared at him with barely-concealed derision.

Abuser.

Were they talking about him? Mike Jenner wasn't an abuser; he was the guy with the big heart and wicked sense of humor who MC'd the Sentinel's holiday party every year and put Gayla Peevey's "I Want a Hippopotamus for Christmas" on a repeating loop and locked the studio door so nobody could change it. Last year, he'd attached a sprig of mistletoe to a plastic St. Patrick's Day hat and walked around kissing everyone, male and female. Everyone loved him at the paper.

Until they didn't.

The wedding clarified his standing. Mike's solution was to simply remove himself from that world and kiss his former friends goodbye. It left him incredibly isolated and lonelier than he'd ever been before.

These days, he could count on one hand the people who were there for him: his parents, his brother, and Roger, his former editor and occasional drinking buddy who was no stranger himself to blackouts and domestic violence charges. Both had experienced loss as a consequence of their addictions, and they took solace together by overindulging in the very vice that caused their problems in the first place. *Fuck it,* Mike thought. *Like Billy Joel said, it's better than drinking alone.*

A rogue wave came out of nowhere, smacking him in the face and forcing salt water down his nose and throat. He stopped and tread water, coughing violently to expel the brine while desperately searching for other waves poised to assault him. He couldn't see anything; the ocean settled down as quickly as it had reared up, flattening into a pane of black glass. The salt water was burning, so Mike unclipped the drinking tube and sipped at it to soothe his throat. Behind him, the coastline was barely visible. It wouldn't be long until he'd lose sight of it completely. Something brushed by him from below, and for a moment he felt pure terror—his body's fight-or-flight response switching on like a current.

Shark? No, not big enough. Probably some random fish.

Although sharks were a scary proposition, the odds of meeting one were still slim. Jellyfish were a bigger concern. They probably couldn't sting him though the wetsuit, but his face and hands were unprotected. He'd been stung on the lip once while he was training and it felt like a hot railroad spike being driven through his mouth. Trying to swim in that kind of pain was the last thing he needed.

Mike flipped onto his back and kicked. It wouldn't be long until he reached the open ocean, and the implications of his actions were becoming very real. At this point, even if he wanted to, he might not physically be able to make it back to shore. *I'm committed now. Committed to ending my life.* Would he know when the time was right, or would he just become so exhausted that he'd welcome death with open arms? Since he was making this up as he went, there were no ready answers. *I could just die right here right now. Dive under and hold myself down until I drown.*

No. Not yet.

He wasn't religious but Alice was a lapsed Catholic and she told him that suicides didn't go to Heaven. Sounded a bit harsh. He wondered if this was true. As his motions slowed and he grew more exhausted, would there be ghostly arms reaching up to drag him down to Hell or some state of Purgatory? It wasn't a particularly pleasant thought, so Mike turned to freestyle again, attempting to re-focus his wandering mind with the mechanics of motion: *reach, pull, kick, breath . . . reach, pull, kick, breath.*

Abuser.

He felt a small but painful tweak in his shoulder and switched to sidestroke to shake it off. He'd hurt the shoulder skiing in Tahoe when the trail he was on unexpectedly dropped out beneath him and he found himself eight feet in the air. When he wiped out, his shoulder took the brunt of it. It wasn't a chronic injury but it did flare up from time to time, especially when he swam. Sidestroke was relaxing but plodding. A stroke for old people who didn't want to get their hair wet.

He lamented how quickly things had gone downhill for him. *One big mistake and I pay for the rest of my life. That's fair? That's justice?* The worst part about all of this was that Mike Jenner didn't deserve it. He was a good guy, and when the final accounting was done he knew he'd leave this earth with more plusses than minuses in his column. Alice would agree with that assessment—he was sure of it—but she'd turned her back and left him anyway.

The sudden veer into violence was a bridge too far for her, and the moment his fist struck the softness of her eye socket, he felt the bond between them break with a sharpness of an icicle snap. He had immediately dropped his hands and backed down, but he knew there was no going back. Maybe he'd changed in some bad way without even realizing it. Sober, he was peaceful enough, but there was a meanness in him that came out when he was deep in the cups. Maybe the demon was always there and the alcohol just fueled its release, Mike didn't really know.

He'd never forget the look of hurt and shock on her face. She didn't cry or speak or make a sound; she simply picked herself up and retreated into the bathroom. He heard the lock click, and ten minutes later there was a knock on the front door and he saw two cops standing on the porch. Next he knew, he was being handcuffed and forcibly escorted to a waiting cruiser outside. He tried to shout out to Alice as they led him away, but she was shielded by another officer and not looking towards him anyway. Sitting in the back of the police car, his arms locked tightly behind him, the enormity of his actions suddenly crashed down on Mike and he fought back tears. In many ways, his journey started that night, many months ago, and tonight that journey would be coming to an end.

As he turned his head to breath, Mike realized that the lights had disappeared and the land along with it. All around him, it was nothing but darkness and infinite expanse of ocean. The barrenness of his surroundings unnerved him. Perhaps people who trekked across deserts or astronauts on the moon could appreciate a similar feeling.

Utter isolation.

Of course this was simply his perception at the surface. Below him, the ocean was teeming with life, but topside it was like a giant eraser had been wiped across the world. Mike knew he'd reach this point eventually; he just didn't expect it to be so profound. And lonely. It also presented a bit of a navigational challenge: without fixed points of reference to guide him, he could be swimming in circles or straight back toward shore. Fortunately, he'd anticipated this and brushed up on his astronomy. Now, he looked to the sky for guidance. *Find the Big Dipper, then follow its handle east. That's the way to open ocean.*

The fundamental notion of celestial navigation was sound, but nature, as she often did, threw a wrench in the gears. Gaggles of low-hanging clouds buzzed overhead and impeded his view of the stars. The muted moonlight had turned everything gunmetal-grey and ugly. Flipping onto his back and floating to conserve energy, Mike did a quick self-check. He was still breathing hard and could feel himself tiring. *Damnit, I should have skipped the hike.* He wasn't prepared to give up yet—he had another couple of miles left in him at least—but there was no denying that his arms and legs were filling with ballast. Better to rest for a spell and wait for the ocean winds to clear the sky then find his bearings. No sense expelling his finite energy swimming back to where he'd started.

Mike's senses were still adjusting to the strange conditions around him. It felt like the ocean was twisting his perceptions. The air was salty and raw, but he could swear he smelled pipe tobacco. A staccato burst of what could have been seals barking, but Mike couldn't tell for sure. Sound was funny out here; unimpeded by natural barriers, it carried for miles, picking up other noises along the way to thoroughly confuse your ears. And the birds . . . of course, the birds. Pretty but ruthless with black doll-eyes. Sometimes they followed him like hungry wolves trailing an injured deer, content to wait for their meal and knowing it would come eventually.

The lights of a distant speedboat racing across the surface, growing fainter and dimmer until they disappeared into the horizon. Wherever there were overpaid athletes, there were boats, and Mike had been to a yacht party or two in his time. He wondered if its passengers had a drink in hand. *What if they came this way? Would I flag them down and tell them some bullshit story about being swept out to sea? Why yes, a drink would help, thank you very much. Manhattan with Wild Turkey, please, and while you're at it, might as well make that a double.*

When the clouds finally passed, the universe opened up. This far from civilization, there were no lights to contaminate the view, and the sky seemed to be everywhere, hypnotizing Mike with its omnipotence. His worshipful gaze eventually found the Big Dipper and he followed its handle to points east. He was glad he'd waited to check his bearings, because he would have chosen a different direction. Taking a sip of water, Mike found that the skein was growing light . . . one of the many countdowns to his eventual demise. Eventually, the drinking water would be gone.

Now?

Not yet.

Mike put his head in the water and started swimming again. Since the moon had shaken off its clouds, he was blessed with a measure of light topside that also provided visibility down to a depth of fifteen, maybe twenty feet. A school of tiny fish passed by, moving together and swerving in perfect synchronicity to avoid him before continuing on their way. Nature could be marvelous like that.

Reach, pull, kick, breath . . . reach, pull, kick, breath . . . He started feeling pretty good again. His energy wasn't beginning to ebb too badly, even if his strokes were slower and pulling less water than he was an hour ago. *Or was it two hours ago?* The bitch of it was that his constant practice had whipped him into pretty damn good shape; maybe the best shape he'd been in since college. By swimming until he was tired then flipping on his back until his batteries recharged, Mike thought he might go even further than he first anticipated.

Maybe forever.

He guessed he was probably about two miles offshore. Covering that kind of distance, he found himself passing through different zones where ocean conditions changed noticeably. The navy blue he saw at the surface faded to black when he looked down, indicating deeper water. While he'd been blessed with relatively calm seas so far, he was now being carried along by increasingly large swells that rose and fell beneath him. For the first time in a long time, he could hear waves crashing, and knew that he must be approaching some reef or shallow that was causing the incoming swells to break. *Guess I'm not as deep as I thought, but this isn't good either.* Waves meant rough water, and that meant expending more energy.

Unfortunately, the swells were taking him for a ride, and he couldn't have changed direction if he wanted to. Strong currents pushed him wherever they wanted to and the waters grew increasingly hectic. The swells were becoming steeper too, and more wave-shaped. Mike found himself suddenly thrust upwards on a rising wave that crested then dropped him down its sheer face and into the trough. His only choice was to submerge under it, and when he surfaced there was another wave coming right behind it. As a surfer, Mike was no stranger to this type of situation, and his instincts took over as he steeled himself for the approaching set.

Dive, surface, quick breath, dive again . . . Over and over, this sequence was repeated as the lines of waves appeared to be endless. Mike lost count at ten. Physically, he felt he was being pushed to the limits of his endurance and his lungs were aching for air. It was like breaking away from the beach all over again, but he was prepared for it then. Now, his resolve had softened after easy swimming in smoother waters. The ocean, unsympathetic to his plight, continued its unrelenting assault, and for the first time that night Mike seriously considered giving up.

I could just let it end right here. It would be easy, I just stop struggling and let the waves take me. Not quite the ending I had in mind but all roads lead to the same place, right?

As if sensing that its point had been made, the ocean settled down, granting Mike a welcome respite. Breathing hard to fill his winded lungs, Mike contemplated what the sudden calmness could signify. He hoped it meant the worst was over, but as a new swell lifted him high, the sight of what was behind it made every cell in his body go cold.

From sea-level, the wave was big as a building and rushing towards him like a circus train. In a split-second, Mike reacted, sucking in a final breath to dive down, but the monster was already upon him, pulling his body into its tractor-beam and flipping his feet up over his head. Suspended upside-down in the curl, Mike prepared to be body-slammed as the wave swelled to an impossible crescendo then pounded down, stuffing him into the washing machine on full spin cycle. The vicious churn tore his fins off and knocked his goggles sideways, filling his eyes with black water. Unrelenting pressure kept him pinned beneath the surface as a thousand different forces clawed at his body from all directions. Like every surfer, Mike had wiped out in big waves before, and the experience taught him some hard-won lessons:

Don't panic.

Find UP then kick like hell.

DON'T PANIC.

He moved his arms and legs to propel an escape, but the water was like a clenched fist around him that refused to open. Its force seemed intent on driving him deeper towards the bottom and holding him down until his fight was gone and the air in his lungs expired. Mike was trying, but his efforts seemed doomed and weak as the waters pummeled him like a child's toy lost in the surf.

For a second time that night, Mike felt life slipping away. He looked for light to guide him topside but there was nothing . . . no down . . . no up . . . just blackness, like being sealed inside an oil drum. The world grew darker and fainter and Mike guessed he was losing consciousness.

So this is the end . . . he thought, but the realization brought him no peace. *This* wasn't the romantic picture he'd held in his mind. Twisting and turning in the underwater vortex, Mike struggled, kicking weakly and trying to claw his way out until the master switch flipped off and everything disappeared.

***

Sunday

When Mike opened his eyes, a million sparkling eyes winked back at him.

What the hell . . . ?

He was bobbing face-up on the surface. There was absolute silence, the kind you almost never experience in life when time stands utterly still and the world shrinks into a tiny circle of focus that fits inside your palm.

I must have passed out . . .

Since he couldn't recall swimming to the surface, the wetsuit and his natural buoyancy must have brought him up. He found his breathing was steady and he wasn't hyperventilating, which probably meant he'd been floating unconscious for some time. Raising his head weakly, he checked the horizon for more waves but there was nothing there. That was good: another giant set surely would have done him in. Instead, it was as if nature, having expended her fury, was content to bow back. The water was flat and glassy and a strange hue more purple than black. Background vibrations emanated from somewhere, stirring the water and buzzing in his head. *That's nothing, just water in your inner ear. That wave must have jammed it in deep.*

As he relaxed and his systems began to power up again, Mike did a self-check. The tip of his nose was frozen, and there was a spot between the wetsuit and his inner thigh where the skin had begun to chafe, making each movement a painful reminder. His tongue was puffy and tasted like salt. No lights or land around him, just water as far as he could see. *Still in the middle of the ocean.* All in all, a bit battered and soggy and definitely tired but still alive. He'd survived and now he could get back to the business of killing himself. The contradiction made him smile, if only for a second.

So now what?

Nobody's going to save me. No paramedics or rescue boats on the way. I can float here like a buoy or put my head down and get back to it.

Now?

Not yet. Closer, though.

Mike raised his vision to the vast canopy of stars overhead but no matter how hard he looked, he couldn't find the Big Dipper. *That's odd.* He wished he'd established more than a handful of navigation points, but, on the other hand, how the hell does a constellation just vanish? Where'd it go? He guessed it was high clouds blocking his view but couldn't detect them. In truth, he was so far out to sea right now that it probably didn't matter which direction he chose. North, south, east west—every course led to the same destination.

Expiration. The Big Sleep. Death.

Coming up with every term he could think of for *death* was a solid (if somewhat morbid) way to keep his mind occupied while he swam. Mike fixed his goggles over his eyes and continued on his way. He tried to feel his movements and establish a rhythm, but his body was telling him he'd gone ten rounds with Andre the Giant. Arms and legs . . . heavy. Exhaustion crept through him like mold and infused into his spine. He wished he hadn't lost the fins—they were at least a force multiplier—and now he was fighting for every stroke. Deliberately slowing his pace, Mike chose to conserve the energy he had left and see how things went before making any major decisions.

Like when to give up.

The water around him suddenly snapped to life as something passed underneath him. Something *big*. Ceasing all motion, he turned upright to tread water. There was a knot in his stomach and his eyes scanned in all directions. Nothing to see but layers and layers of obsidian ocean. *It's probably a fish or seal … maybe even a porpoise.* Those were the safe, benign answers, his mind refusing to consider the more dangerous alternatives. In a flash, the entity appeared again, making several quick runs back and forth, close enough to brush his legs and send shockwaves through the water.

Whatever was below the surface, it was fast and it was sizable and it was obviously checking him out. Mike glanced at the shark band on his wrist but there was no display, no light . . . no way to tell if it was working. *Fucking waste of money.* Avoiding any sudden movements that might draw the beast's attention, Mike let the surface current roll him into a dead man's float so he could stare downwards. He strained to see movement or make out any discernible shapes—a head, a fin, a tail—that might offer a clue, but there was nothing.

Whatever it is, it has instinct and intelligence. That much was obvious. *But what could it be, and more importantly, what does it want with me?* If it was an aggressive predator, there wouldn't be much Mike could do about it. He was out of his element and the creature was on its home turf. It would dictate the terms of battle, and if it decided to make him a meal, the best he could hope for was quick death.

For now, at least, the world was still. Mike continued to float as seconds became minutes, all senses on heightened alert for any further encroachments. But there was nothing. In a way, that was even worse because it left him suspended, his imagination running wild. Maybe, he hoped, the creature had become disinterested and swum off. Or, maybe it was biding its time and creating distance to gear up for a final, fatal run at him . . . gathering speed before rushing up from lightless depths with a maniac smile and jaws full of diamond-cutters perfectly evolved to tear through flesh and bone.

He'd read about a great white shark in Australia that had been tagged by scientists to track its movements and habits. Everything was fine until the signal suddenly went dead. The researchers were perplexed and couldn't figure out what had happened until the tracker unexpectedly washed up on shore. Analyzing the data, the researchers speculated that the shark had been attacked and ingested by another unidentified marine carnivore big enough to swallow a ten-foot shark whole.

To Mike, stories like this confirmed that nobody *really* knew what creatures could be hiding in the ocean depths. He'd studied the topography of the shoreline and knew that, at a certain point, you'd reach the rugged edge of the continental shelf where the ocean suddenly plunged two miles down into otherworldly darkness. If he'd reached that point, then the bottom had fallen out and there could be *anything* below him. Floating out here in the middle of nowhere by himself, he knew that he had no protection, no safe harbor, and the only small comfort he could take was that it seemed the beast had moved on.

Cautiously, Mike extended his arms and legs to swim again, this time employing a modified breaststroke that kept his head above water. Gliding, he remained vigilant for any sound, sight or movement that might foreshadow an attack. It was silly, really, that he'd have any fear at this point, but when you trespass in an alien environment, the fear is hard-coded. Three-hundred thousand years of instinct don't just disappear because your will to live has ebbed.

A strange moan rose from somewhere in the fog, an unnatural, eerie sound that at first sounded like a dog but took on an almost human timbre as it continued. Once, twice, then a final haunting wail that

Mike imagined to be full of pain but was probably just his mind and the weirdness of this place fucking with him. Regardless, it sent a deep chill through his body.

Whale. That must be a whale.

How could it be anything else?

Mike remained motionless and waited for the sound to come again, but after listening for several minutes there was nothing. To carry on, his course was either straight down or straight ahead, so Mike chose the latter and began moving again, indifferent to any sense of navigation. He had entered a new zone, and the water here was placid, more like a lake than ocean. *No waves, thank God.* Under different circumstances, the conditions would have actually been pleasant for swimming, and he continued undisturbed for some period of time while his mind kept itself occupied sifting through his all-time hero Joe Montana's total passing yardage by season (college and pro). He liked Steve Young, too, but Montana had always been his guy. Around him, the ocean's deliberate calmness was almost welcoming, as though it was inviting him to keep swimming . . . to go even further. He was respectful of death but not scared of it (at least that's what he kept telling himself), and the ocean's strange, seductive power kept pulling him forward toward their final rendezvous.

I'll be so tired by then that it will be just like going to sleep. Or it could be terrifying . . .

Now?

Not yet. But almost.

Swimming on autopilot and lost in thought, Mike barely noticed the swirling clump of seaweed at first. It was tangled and black in the moonlight and the only tangible thing he'd seen in some time. Even though he knew it wasn't possible, Mike couldn't shake the feeling that it was following him. *That can't be . . .even without the fins, I'm still faster than the current.* Yet, there it was, floating along the surface, still but not immobile, propelled by some unseen force that matched his pace as he moved through the water. Intent on pulling away, Mike dug in, paddling harder and demanding more power from his fatigued body. But he couldn't seem to shake the strange mass. No matter how fast he swam, the clump of seaweed was right there, an unwelcome companion that maintained a steady distance at the edge of his wake but never completely disappeared from sight.

Mike wasn't sure if he should be intrigued or disturbed so he changed course and began scissor-kicking towards the mass. Perhaps sensing his shift, it retreated at first, maintaining a steady twenty-foot buffer between them. *That's not seaweed . . . it's responding to my movements.* But what the fuck could it be? A group of jellyfish? A squid with its head caught up in some abandoned netting? Every instinct was pulling him in the opposite direction, but Mike let his curiosity push him on. Cautiously, he drew closer . . . closer . . . closer until the object was just outside his reach. He extended an arm to grasp a floating tendril and figure out just what the fuck this thing could be.

All at once, the seaweed shook violently and began to rise out of the water. Something beneath it was pushing it up. Mike sculled backward and stared in fascination. The low-lying clouds had reappeared to wrap the moon in grey bandages, but even in diminished light there was no mistaking what he was seeing. Mike gasped as his fevered mind tried to process the spectacle that had risen from the depths to present itself before him.

It was a woman. A girl, really. Staring back at him.

Her sudden appearance shocked him. He strained in the darkness to make out the contours of her face, barely visible beneath the quivering mass of black coils. The figure was silent in her contemplation of him. Then, in a split-second, she pitched forward and started swimming, her body undulating across the surface. Mike was struck by her legs, which were not separate appendages but fused together into a single trunk. Her feet were misshapen and joined at the heels, pointing out at unnatural angles to create the impression of a fin.

Like a tail. A fish's tail.

Then, like completing a puzzle box, things clicked into place.

A mermaid . . . she looks like a mermaid.

The figure circled back to move in his direction before diving down. Mike plunged his head into the water to watch as she swam fast and deep then disappeared from view. He kept his head submerged as long as he could but there was no sign of her. Pulling up and gasping for air, unreality washed over him like an arctic storm. *What the fuck??!!*

The mermaid-thing broke the surface again, shooting out of the water to an impressive height and flipping twice before plunging back beneath the black waves. She reminded Mike of the porpoises at Sea World. He could feel her form pass below him as she sped past and breached the water again—closer this time—reaching an apex at least fifteen feet in the air in a display of raw, animalistic power. Her proximity enabled Mike to see her much more clearly. She was unclothed and bare-breasted with luminescent white skin stained by a dark film. Her presence filled the air with an odious smell, one that reeked of long-forgotten layers of rot and decay dredged from the ocean's bottom.

It seemed the world had veered into the surreal as Mike tried to make sense of the sudden appearance of a woman (or whatever she was) with a half-formed tail in the middle of the ocean. The most likely explanation was that Mike had taken complete leave of his senses. *I'm hypoxic . . . exhausted . . . delusional even. This can't be happening . . .*

But his sense were telling him a different story and there was no denying the physical presence of the creature now racing circles around him or her stench or the splash of cold water in his face when she dove next to him.

Why is she here? Why me?

He realized that thoughts of suicide had left his head completely. How could he leave this world when it was showing him something secret and magnificent? There must be a reason for that.

Confused and awed, he waited breathlessly for her return, every nerve electric and on edge. He thought the anticipation might kill him, saving him the trouble of doing it himself. A rolling boil at the surface indicated movement below and in an instant she burst out of the water at his side, close enough to impact Mike with sudden force. Her misshapen but strangely beautiful body hung in the moonlight above him, contorting and twisting, before she sliced the water like a Ginsu and sped straight down into unseen depths.

Mike gasped and reached for his injured side. He didn't have time to recover or contemplate this concerning turn of events because she was surfacing to speed at him again. He tried to brace himself but she impacted into his upper body and spun him in the water. Turning to make another high-speed pass, she headed directly at him before veering off at the last second, her tail-legs lashing at him with the force of a stallion's kick. His shoulder instantly went numb. The creature's provocations were more frenzied now, and to Mike it seemed she was everywhere at once, like there were ten of her all around him. She moved with such force and velocity that Mike couldn't respond or adequately protect himself. *I'm a sitting duck.*

What started as an almost playful exchange had metastasized into something sinister. She passed below him like a torpedo, swimming hard to create distance and then pivoting back to head directly towards him. Her motions were almost delicate, like a water-gazelle bounding across an open plain, before she plunged below the surface and out of sight. He searched desperately, but before he could react there was a sudden and massive impact from below as she propelled herself into him, upending him completely and carrying his body into the air. Gracelessly, he crashed back into the hard water, the pain exploding with such ferocity that it almost caused him to black out.

Dazed and battered, Mike floated face-up. His eyes, wide open and unblinking, stared up at the universe. *Whereza Big Dipper? Gotta find it an star swimmin' agin . . .*

The creature's aggression was sudden and brutal. There was nothing he could do about it, and in that moment, Mike felt closer to death than he ever had before. As he waited for her to return, an impending sense of dread spider-walked up his spine. Every noise sent involuntary spasms through his broken body.

Pain wasn't supposed to be part of the plan. If I wanted pain, I could have killed myself in a thousand different ways.

The clouds had melted away again and the moon shone through, beautiful and indifferent to the sufferings of a solitary man in the water. Through the sea-air, Mike could vaguely see something coming towards him. He blinked to clear the saltwater clouding his vision, and what appeared made Mike gasp and then question whether he'd lost whatever remained of his sanity.

It was Alice.

She floated across the surface of the water, her bare feet dragging across the tips of the whitecaps. Her robes were white-gold and bright as a sunrise. Her face was young, like that day they first met at Cal, and she was smiling at him. There was no anger or pain or hurt there. Her expression was pure benevolence and he knew in an instant that his beloved had to come back to him. She would rescue him from this fool's errand.

"Michael," she breathed.

"Alice," he responded.

His heart swelled and there was nothing in his mind except her. She moved towards him and extended her arms. He had no choice but to go to her. Gripping her tightly in a warm embrace, his anguish was a distant memory . . . his plans of suicide forgotten. All that mattered was this moment, right now, and being together with Alice.

Everything's going to be OK . . .

Alice moaned and arched backwards, her chestnut hair dipping into the water. Mike closed his eyes and leaned in for a kiss but in an instant Alice's body went cold and slippery and a wretched stench filled the air. His face right next to hers, he looked on in horror as her features began to contort and liquify until Alice was transformed into something primitive and ugly. Its eyes were filmy and a strange yellow color. Barnacles covered its mouth and lips. A thin white companion fish hung limply from one cheek, its jaws sunk into the muddy flesh. And the roman nose, of course. Even through the filth and decay, that feature was still prominent in her profile.

In that singular moment, a revelation slashed through Mike's brain, and he *knew*.

"Emily?" he whispered. "Emily Guindon?"

There was a flash of recognition as they lizard-film dropped from her eyes and she looked almost human. He was struck by the sadness he saw there. She opened her mouth and howled, that same sound he had heard earlier but much louder . . . an unnatural wailing full of hunger and desire and pain.

Not a whale's call.
The howl of a predator.

Abruptly, her head snapped up and she pulled him into a death-hold. The mermaid-thing's entire countenance changed as they came face-to-face, and the look in her burning eyes was one of pure malice. Like snakes, the coils of her hair began to spread out and slither up his feet and ankles to bind them tight. Locked in her supernatural embrace, Mike struggled weakly but found he was paralyzed.

When she dove, he couldn't even expand his chest to gasp in a last, full breath of air. She sped downwards, dragging him into a fathomless abyss that grew colder and colder and darker and darker until he had no choice but to stop struggling and let the surrounding blackness envelop him.

Knowing this was the end, Mike didn't see his life flash before his eyes or think of his family or even Alice. No, his feeling was one of overwhelming terror.

I don't want to die.
I want to live . . .

But it was too late for him now and in the dying embers of his mind a final thought formed before the water rushed in and extinguished what was left of Mike Jenner for good:

I was gonna write the book . . . I . . .

Then everything switched off and the only thing he knew was darkness and decay as the rusalka dragged his body down, down, down to whatever fate awaited him in the desolate depths below.

About the Author

Jonathan Jewett is a writer, musician, and technology professional whose writing credentials span from business to horror. His first book cracked the Top 10 among business bestsellers on Amazon, and ***Evil Chose You*** is his first novel in the horror genre. A lifelong fan of horror books and movies, Jonathan's stories range from monsters and the macabre to dystopian futures where technology goes very wrong and brings our worst nightmares to life. A native of Massachusetts, Jonathan currently resides in New England with his family and rambunctious French Bulldog.

Visit jonathanjewett.net to sign up for sneak peeks of upcoming stories, product giveaways and more cool stuff.